WESTPOINT

1

'Welcome to Malhangers,' he said. 'You're here for two reasons, two only. You've shown talent in your field, and you're members of the Family. I'm not going to speak for long before I hand you over to your Head of Year, Miss Doubleday.'

I knew this meant he would talk for half an hour; head teachers are like that. I settled down in my seat, sucked a mint.

'Here at Malhangers we're proud of our alumnae. This school has produced some of the finest politicians, financiers, lawyers and civil servants in the land, people who have gone to the very top of their profession. They run the country. They govern the judiciary. They are policy wonks, town planners, newspaper editors, TV producers. And what, ladies and gentlemen, do they all have in common, apart from being products of this fine, ancient establishment?'

He paused for dramatic effect. 'They're all crooks, the finest crooks other people's money can buy and this is why you're here, to join that elect group. So let us all stand and say together the school motto.'

We rose, pushed back our chairs, and stared at each other shyly, knowing those around us would be friends for life, the Family. It was a family we would never be able to leave. Then we chanted as one. **'Serve Yourself First'**

I can't say for sure, but I think I spotted a tear running down Miss Doubleday's cheek. So why was I at Malhangers? What had I done to show such promise? Let's go back to the very beginning.

2

I stole £30 Million. I might also tell you "how" but not in too much detail. I don't want to lead you astray. I was lucky in those early days but stupid. You're probably smart but not so lucky. That's just the way it is, sorry. Believe me that's the best way. My honest advice, it's always best if you stay on the right side of the law. Not as much fun but unless you want to spend a lifetime breaking in to a sweat whenever the phone rings then avoid crime. It's a profession where, as the saying goes, many are called but few are chosen.

First, I don't categorise myself as a thief, which would be a terrible accusation to make against me. A number of people have made that accusation and it would be difficult to contradict them but, in my mind, I am as innocent as a lamb.

I want you to believe that, even though other people don't. I know that I took something that didn't belong to me, but I did this out of the best of motives. I committed this crime with a pure heart, a dumb, misinformed teenage heart but still a pure one. I stole the money out of love, misguided but love all the same. It's a philosophical question, is it right to do the wrong thing with the right mind?

There wasn't a girl, well there was, sort off. There's always a girl. Without her I would never have met him. I'm not gay, at least I don't think so, although the jury is out. I wouldn't have a problem with if I were. I just want you to know that this was not a crime of passion. It was just that her father was so, I don't know what, he was just "so".

He was everything I wanted to be but wasn't. He knew things: how to dress, make a joke without saying a word, put a

stranger at ease, do the Times crossword, eat a gherkin, play croquet without cheating, important stuff like that – especially the
croquet. He could simultaneously knot a bow tie and put on his
cufflinks at the same time, try it. It's difficult. It's now one of the
basic entry-level tests for training as a helicopter pilot.

Above all he knew how to make money, a pile of it. The sort
of pile that you keep hidden in mountains and get dragons to
guard. At least, I thought this was his forte. He lived in a big house,
and people who live in big houses in quiet roads with swimming
pools and lawns that stretch down to the pavement, and who wear
loud Hawaiian shirts, always know how to make money. Don't
they? Not too sure about the Hawaiian shirt thing.

The answer in this case was 'no' but at the time I didn't know
that. In fact, I didn't know very much at all. That is the problem
with being sixteen, we know a lot but less than we imagine, and
we imagine so much more than we know.

The house was enormous, the garage bigger than the flat
where I lived. I have a thing about garages. You'll find that out if
you stick with me. I don't mean garage music either, in fact I don't
know the difference between garage and house, music-wise. But
this guy had a big swinging garage, that's for sure.

I almost didn't knock on the door. It was a door built to
intimidate, to say "go away unless you're one of us". It was huge,
arched, and wooden with a brass knocker in the shape of a Greek
god, Hermes I believe. I sometimes wonder what its like to be
a Greek god one moment and then a doorknob. I hope they get
counselling over that because it's a difficult adjustment to make.
I hovered in the doorway, paralysed with fear. It would not be the
first time that knockers threw me.

The door flew opened. A man, sporting a green cashmere
cardigan, which I thought was a bit young for him, looked down
on me smiling in an absent-minded sort of way. It was love at first
sight. Well, for me.

'Who are you?' I said.

'Shouldn't I be asking that? I live here.'

'Just wanted to know I'm at the right house.'

'Who are you looking for?'

'I can't tell you that.'

He started to close the door. I stuck my foot in the doorway, not literally of course, just metaphorically. 'It's logical, isn't it?'

'Logical?'

'If I told you who I was looking for you could say that you were that person even if you weren't'

He creased his forehead in an exaggerated way, which made me laugh. 'I suppose so, yes. "Ok, I'll tell you who I am. My name's Peters. You trying to sell me something?"

'No tea towels, no life assurance, no religion. Do I look like a salesman?' then I added, 'why did you open the door?'

He glanced up at the security lens which I'd missed; of course, there was a camera. 'I was bored. You'd been there for a while. I was curious.' He looked at me. I was wearing scruffy jeans, torn at the knees, trainers, 'So why are you on my doorstep causing a nuisance?'

'You have a daughter?'

'You mean Arabella? I understand now, you could have easily mistaken me for her. You're not her boyfriend, are you?'

'No.' I took a step backwards, outraged,

'And why not? She's very pretty.'

I was outmanoeuvred by him. 'I didn't mean that she's not, you know, pretty, only that I'm here about something else.'

'And what would that be?'

'Maths'

'What do you mean?'

'Numbers, sums, proofs, probabilities, sequences, the poetry of logical ideas'

'That's good that last line, I like that, "the poetry of logical ideas"'

'I stole it from Einstein.'

'Did you now?' He stared into space for an infinite moment, scratched his ear. Later, when I got to know him, I realised this was a habit of his, the scratching of his ear – the left one to be precise, especially when he didn't know what to do. I tried to adopt the habit myself but never really mastered it. I've never really had an itchy ear. I pressed my point.

'We're maths buddies, in the same maths set. We're supposed to work together. Didn't Ari say anything about it?'

'Ari? Is that what you call her?'

'Yup, at school. She's Ari. Didn't she tell you?'

'No, she doesn't really talk to me about school, or maths, or her life, or anything really. In fact, she very rarely talks to me at all.'

He turned and called in mock solemnity. 'Ari, there's a young man here to see you, your Maths Buddy.' He mouthed silently to me, 'and you are?'

'Zac … I'm Zac.'

He yelled back into the hallway. 'He's called, what's your name?'

'Zac.'

'He's called Zac.'

A minute passed when neither of us said anything. He broke the embarrassing silence. 'What's Zac short for?'

'I have no idea.'

Ari stuck her head round the door. She took one look at me and went bright red. I think I did too, to be fair. I'm not sure why I caused this reaction in her. Either she fancied me or, quite simply, I embarrassed her: mind you, it could have been both because neither is mutually exclusive. I think it was fair to say that I definitely fancied Ari, but this was not one of those young-love scenarios. It was just because she was seriously pretty and sweet, and I was a bag of hormonal jellyfish.

3

When Mrs Moon, our maths teacher, put us together as maths buddies I was pleased, although I could see that Ari was mortified. I'm not cool. I read somewhere that the secret to being cool is to not try to be cool. Then magically you will become cool. Just don't try, that's the secret. Maybe I've tried not to be cool too much because I've succeeded. I'm definitely not cool. Maybe I'm just too hot to be cool, perhaps not even that. Anyway, all this trying not to be cool is working me in to a sweat. Maybe because Ari was so hot.

'Oh, it's you,' she said with as much enthusiasm as if I were a plate of broccoli. I know she doesn't like broccoli because she told me once. It was, at that time, one of the few things I knew about her, other than she struggled with simultaneous equations, which I really like in a sad sort of way. I guess I was a kind of vegetable to her, something she would toy with, push around her plate but never really relish. I was a human broccoli.

'You'd better come in,' she said.

It was not much of an invitation, half-hearted really but I took it. I slipped past Peters, before he changed his mind, and was led into the dining room, and this was how I made it into the Peters' household. My life had changed but I didn't realise it. How many moments are like that in our lives? Something very insignificant happens yet it changes everything. Perhaps it was because they had a dining room, and ate in it, rather than at the kitchen table or in front of the telly, or on the floor.

At one stage, before I messed everything up, I almost became a member of the Peters family. I was nearly part of their beautiful and ordered world. It was to be a brief moment of sunlight in my shabby existence. I didn't fall in love with Ari, not straight away.

The person I really fell in love with, to begin with, was her father Peters, but not in some sick pervy kind of way; but only because he was a good man and a friend to me. Also, for the psychoanalysts among you, and I guess there are many who've read enough articles in women's mags or seen You Tube videos to essentially qualify as a psychoanalyst, I don't have a dad. He was a sort of idealised father. He always likes to be known by his surname, Peters. I guess its some public schoolboy kind of thing, either way I like it. All this first name terms business gets my goat. Not that I have a goat but if I did, it wouldn't last long.

Then there was Ari's grandmother, Lilly. More of her later, as they say. I loved Lilly and she me, I'm sure. Of course, I'm not allowed to see any of them now, except at pre-approved times, under strict supervision, monitored. I'm poor so I have to follow the rules, their rules. At least that's what they think.

4

When I cycled back that evening, I found that Paul had forgotten to put the keys back under the flowerpot by the front door. He forgets quite often. It's not a very secret hiding place but it does for us. If you want to rob us, that's where to look, just don't expect to find much; and if you're feeling generous, a tip would be appreciated.

But I warn you, Paul's a copper. He does shift work, late at night, undercover stuff, nothing exciting just keeping an eye on petty crooks in pubs and clubs, pickpockets, handbag snatchers. Sometimes he sits in cars for hours on end watching houses, logging when people leave or arrive. Often, he doesn't know why he's watching people, just has to do it, need to know basis only. He's too far down the food chain. Not even fast food.

He never knows when he's going to come home. When he does pitch up, he's so beat he doesn't think straight, so rather than leaving the keys for me, he puts them in his pocket and goes to sleep on the sofa, a half-eaten take-away on the floor. I can't wake him up either no matter how hard I try banging on the door, especially when he's had a glass or two to help calm himself down.

We have a garage. I told you I have an interest in garages. I've put an old mattress in it and a sleeping bag. It does for me when I'm locked-out and need to camp down for the night. Paul's always beside himself in the morning with guilt and shame. 'I'm sorry mate, I'm so really sorry. What am I like?'

Neither of us tells anyone. It's our big secret, the kid in the garage. We don't want the social services round. What is it about people who work in the social services? They all have beards and wear synthetic clothes. And that's just the women.

It would be bad for his career, a policeman neglecting his

own ward, and for me I couldn't stand a foster family, and I'm not a cute kid so I probably wouldn't get one anyway. I'm like that song, you know, a "teenage dirt bag". I've practised my cute smile but believe me it just doesn't work. I look deranged. Also, it serves me to have Paul feeling guilty. It's an emotion I can use.

There's no light in the garage and that suits me fine. I always feel safer in the dark, and then there's my old friend, Fibonacci, the mathematician. He'd died around 1250 but I still felt close to him. Dead friends are the best ones ever. They don't answer back. You don't have to send them cards on their birthday, or Christmas presents. Also, you get the tv control. Pizza for one is cheaper. So, a bit of free advice. If you want a friend, make sure they're dead. The only problem is, they're rubbish at sleepovers.

Time for a major confession. Nothing serious. I'm not into boy bands or anything. I like numbers. I had this discussion with my mate Matt at school the other day.

'Matt, tell me, honest – am I a nerd?'

He stuck a pencil up his nose, always the sophisticate, 'In my opinion, no, mate – you're not a nerd.'

'But I like maths and stuff.'

'You're more a sort of Indie.'

'Ah thanks,' Indie sounded cool to me.

'What am I then?' he asked warily.

Matt liked to wear baggy clothes and army stuff and was growing his hair long and greasy. 'You're a bit Grunge mate, you know, when you're not at school.'

'So does that mean we can't be friends?' he asked.

'It'll cause issues, but no probs.'

'You talk such cock.'

'Yeah, I know,' I replied, 'I'm fluent in speaking cock. Shame you can't do a GCSE in it.'

I suppose the only reason I look Indie is that I buy all my clothes from second-hand shops, not the posh second-hand shops like the ones in Notting Hill. I'm talking South London council estate. It's all I can afford. Here's the big confession, please don't be shocked. It's not that bad, not as if I collect guns, troll celebrities on the internet, or am a member of the young Conservatives.

My thing is, and it's important you know, if you're at all interested in me, and there's no reason you should be, except that crooks are sometimes interesting, is that I find comfort in counting, but not timetables or anything like that.

I'm not into timetables. I did have a frisky liaison once, for a short time, with some local bus schedules but I never really got into them. It was a bit shallow, and to be frank less of a mathematical sequence introducing order and negative entropy into a chaotic universe, and more a work of fiction, a big fat lie. I was dating a tart.

I like sequences, especially the one where the next number is the sum of the previous two. Fibonacci compared it to rabbits breeding; maybe they were genetically enhanced freaky rabbits because they never died, maybe it was the only way you could talk about fornication politely in those days. I'm a bit worried that he used to think about sex though. Mathematicians should live in a world of numbers, cold showers, and sharpened pencils. I try to work out the sequence my head, a bit like counting sheep, only it's more fun with rabbits. Sheep are so last century, even if they do have electronic dreams themselves.

Matthew told me his hobby was masturbation. No wonder he used to look so tired in the mornings at school. It's like everyone does it, apart from the Pope of course, but Matthew took it to new heights. He told me that www stood for world-wide-wank. I believed him for a while, well a few nanoseconds. Every time, he entertained himself he would paint a stone white and put it in his back garden. He told his mom he was making a zen garden. There were a few big stones. He told me that it was a bit zen in that whatever angle of the garden you stood at one wank was hidden.

When I'm in the garage, I hang up my school uniform, so it doesn't fall on the oily floor and then I slip into the sleeping bag. I keep it in a plastic bag, so the mice don't get to it. I don't like mice droppings. They'll just pooh anywhere. I got friends like that, practically incontinent., turning skid marks into an art form. Roll over Jackson Pollock.

The thing is that the garage is not just a place, it's a state of mind. It's where I belong, where I can hide, where I'm safe. No-one can disturb me there. Then I start counting: 0,1,1,2,3,5,8,13, 21, 34. Truth, is I remember most of the lower ones now but when I get to around 701,408,733 I give up and fall asleep, it's funny having numbers as friends. I know they're numbers not rabbits, it's just a comfort that's all. I'm glad they're not rabbits. I don't like bunnies. They can be really vicious, must be all that pent-up sexual frustration. I've got friends like that too. In fact, all of them.

Sometimes when I can't sleep I go on the internet, for some reasons I can get next door's connection for free, so I hitch a lift on that. I go to a specialist site. I'm a bit addicted to it. I know what you're thinking and it's not what you think, not porn, not naked girls playing brass instruments in a bath full of custard - but if you find a site like that, drop me a line.

What I like is maths. There's a forum I like, people like me. We do encryption puzzles. There's one guy I speak to a lot, Blue. He's a computer science student at Westpoint, a military academy in the USA, one whose not been brain damaged by a pillowcase. Sometimes I like to spook him by breaking his encryption puzzles, normally they're timed and if you get them wrong there's a rude Anglo-Saxon word at the end.

Blue's cool. I want to be Blue, and not just blue. I am by the way, just a dull background radiation of sadness. It's hormonal I'm sure. By the time I'm in my mid-thirties I'll feel happy, maybe a bright yellow. Then I'll get married, have children of my own and turn blue again.

5

When I got back from Ari's house that afternoon my uncle was up to his usual tricks. He won't let me have a set of keys of my own. I know why. It's because of his girlfriend Sharon. She's round there from time to time. They don't want me walking in on them, and you know what? It's something I'd rather not think about, or hear for that matter, so I don't really mind.

The thing about number rabbits is they're a lot quieter than the real thing. I'm not sure which would be worse, seeing Paul naked or Sharon but the idea of them making out on kitchen surfaces is too much for my adolescent psyche, especially when last night's Indian takeaway is slowly congealing in the sink. People don't realise how vulnerable we teenagers are, fantasy is so much better than reality.

I got back from Ari's and the door was closed, curtains shut, key gone. I knocked and called through the letter box. No reply. I went to the burger shop and bought a packet of chips and a coke, just checking out of the corner of my eye that Jamie Oliver wasn't hiding somewhere ready to pounce with one of his school dinners. Thou shall eat an olive salad. Doesn't he know that one of the fundamental rules of the Pythagorean order is to abstain from beans?

When I went back to the garage I made sure no-one could see I was in there, slipped in via the back passage. Something I'm not interested in by the way. I had a pee up against the wall. Like most boys my age, I like to count prime numbers when I pee – 2,3,5,7,11,13,17,19,23. If I don't get up to at least 23 I feel it's been a psycho-pee or, at worst, a just-in-case pee: but 23 is respectable. Once I got to 67 but that was a freak. I don't know how that happened, but prime number peeing at that level is outside the curve. Maybe I'd gone a bit wild and had too many alco-pops in the rec after a school disco. Then I settled down for the night.

Lying in my bed, I thought of Ari, not in any pervy way, well just a bit, can't be helped. One of the other rules of the Pythagorean order is to never touch a white cock. I'm afraid I've broken that rule every day for years, that's what socks are for, yes? I guess that's why Paul's so rubbish at maths. He's an old bean who touches his cock quite regularly. Plato probably never wore socks though. I guess he had sandals.

I liked how perfect Ari's home was, everything ordered, beautiful, clean. It was a home where thought had gone into every detail, not thrown together from second-hand shops like mine. Designers had been consulted; professional decorators employed. It was Scandinavian chic with a touch of art deco. Mine was recycled seventies pine with a touch of cigarette burn.

Paul had a dog once, a bull terrier called Mince. She stayed in all day, scratched up the doors and the furniture. She used to pee on the kitchen floor. Paul didn't mind. He said it was a good thing the dog peed on the floor, otherwise it would never get cleaned. As it was, the kitchen was bleached down at least three times a week. It should have been washed seven days a week but let's not dwell on that. I can't imagine a dog ever peeing in Ari's home, not in the way that it was sort of a norm. It wasn't a dog-piss kind of a house. I don't think they do dog-piss in Scandinavia; but if they did, it would be really cool, and everybody would have some.

Eventually, Mince went to a new home where she was loved and given the freedom to urinate on the next-door neighbour's lawn, just like every other dog. I missed Mince for a little while. The kitchen floor got grubbier and grubbier. I considered pissing on it myself but one day I discovered Paul on his knees, scrubbing it down; as the French say, "cherchez la femme." That's where I first met Sharon, in the kitchen, a glass of sweet German white wine in her hand. She was standing in a particularly polished part of the kitchen, and Paul glanced at me, a warning, 'don't mention the dog piss'. I smiled. It's not a place I would ever have stood.

Aside from canine troubles, Ari never had to sleep in a garage either. She missed out on a character-building formative experience, learning how to make yourself comfortable in the most unpromising of circumstances is a useful skill. I suppose she was disadvantaged in a way, never having had the genuine garage experience.

Having a difficult childhood, so people say, can pay real dividends later in life when it comes to dealing with the hard blows and getting through them. I'm not sure I believe them when they say that. I think it's just something that people say, if they've survived that is.

Peters was uber-cool He told me that he wanted to be me when he grew up, and I believed him. I believed everything he told me. I wanted to. He offered to pay me to mow his lawn. I decided to take him up on that. It would be an excuse to go round every Sunday afternoon, to see Ari. I told myself that it was Ari that I had a crush on, though of course it wasn't. It wasn't her I came to see at all, although she did look gorgeous. The money was good too. I was saving up. One day I wanted to have enough to buy a really big house like Peters, well maybe just a Hermes doorknob.

I made sure I always arrived in time for lunch. I like the definition of being rich as eating three times a day. Paul gives me lunch money from time to time, but he forgets more often than he remembers. Occasionally, I help myself from his wallet. I leave a little note to tell him. He doesn't seem to mind. I wonder whether he ever notices. But he is like, you know, a policeman so he should notice, or at least work out whose taking his money. His detective training should kick in.

Anyway, that night, the first after I had met Ari's family, I fell to sleep straight away, unaware of the corner I had turned in my life; the sleep of the innocent, totally unaware of what I had walked in to.

6

Paul woke me up in the morning. He crouched down beside me and shook my elbow. I crawled out of my sleeping bag and trod warily back to the flat. Sharon had left for work. He made a fry-up whilst I showered. Paul was a bit sheepish which was good. Guilt is always useful, as I've said. I can exploit it. 'I need some money for my finger.'

The school uses our fingers as biometric ID for lunch money. It's scary really. Is there a central database somewhere with all our fingerprints on it? Will some enterprising PhD student dig up the lunch records of all psychopaths or prime ministers and point out that they all ate far too many chilly flavoured mushrooms, or skipped lunch more often than others? Paul looked at me suspiciously.

'You had that last week.'

His detective training had not been in vain.

'School food's not cheap, not since Jamie Oliver's been on the case.'

'How much?'

'I think a tenner should do it.'

He took a note from his pocket and handed it to me. We both knew it wouldn't be spent on food.

'All right?'

He kind of knew that he was being conned. He is a police officer after all, but it was the least path of resistance.

When I arrived at school I got in to trouble straight away. After the register, Mr Thorpe, my overweight, uncharismatic form teacher, hovered over me. 'Where's your homework Zac?'

My heart sank.

'What homework would that be, sir?' I added the "sir" to

annoy him.

'You know what I mean, 'Your English essay.'

'I 'ain't done it, sir. I'll do it tonight, sir.' If they're deter-mined to find me a social problem, I'd might as well drop my "h's".

Sadly, that didn't cut it, so I got a C1. The school loves things called Consequences – C1, C2s and C5s. A C1 is not too bad. It's more of a badge of honour. If you don't have at least a few C1s on your end of term report you lose all street cred. Besides, Paul never reads my reports. I intercept them. A C1 means you have to stay in the library during the lunchtime break but that's ok by me. The library is a safe place. No chance of being hung upside down naked in a tree or beaten to a pulp by over-enthusiast teenage psycho-paths. Happens in the library too, of course, but rarely. Usually in the moral philosophy section, but no-one ever goes there.

The important thing about the library is to never catch anyone's eye, because invariably the more nervous kids are there, and if you catch their eye then you're linked, one of them. It's not a good idea to be one of them. Always better to commit an act of mindless random violence at the beginning of every school term then you're safe, people leave you alone. A C5 means you get put into a time machine and handed over to the Stazis.

The Consequence of my uncle spending his day on the underground chasing pick pockets, and then chasing Sharon round the bedroom, or the kitchen, means that I can't do my homework. It's not a serious consequence but it's a real one. I felt dog-tired throughout the day, didn't get much sleep, me, and the rodents. There is a downside to garage life. I wrote my English essay in the lunchtime.

I scribbled a few lines on Zeno's paradox, that we all need to move through an infinite series of reducing spaces. That was why I couldn't do my homework, as basically all movement is the-oretically impossible, to pick up my pen I had to move through a foot of space but to get even halfway there I'd have had to move at least half a foot and so on to infinity, and as there's an infinity of page to write in I'd found it impossible to do my homework. Yeah, consequence that Mr Thorpe. I know there's now a complex mathematical solution to this paradox but sometimes problems are so much more secure to hang on to than solutions. A problem is a friend for a life, but a solution just leads you to the next problem.

7

That first afternoon when I went to see Ari her mum, "call me Anne", asked me to stay for lunch. I think they were being polite and were probably a bit surprised when I agreed. That's always the problem with polite people. It's impossible to tell what they really mean. If someone comes to Paul's flat and we're watching a really cool film we would tell them to bog off, or similar words, and come back in a few hours; or we would sit them in the corner and tell them that if they made a sound they were dead meat. Then we'd turn up the sound just to reinforce the fact that their arrival was a blatant abuse of human rights.

This was not the case at Ari's house, oh no. The TV would be switched off; 'how lovely to see you. Would you like a cup of tea?' This was middle-class speak for, 'Oh crap, now we'll never find out who made off with Desdemona's handkerchief'.

And whilst I'm on a roll I want to say a few words about how middle-class people say thank you. In Paul's flat if you gave you them your spare kidney you'd just get an appreciative grunt, or if they wanted to make a super-human effort they'd just say 'ta'. But in Ari's home, you'd arrive with a small offering – say a dead mouse – and they'd say, 'thank you sooooo much" as if they really meant it. You'd feel good about yourself, the whole deceased rodent idea had worked.

All that time you'd had a niggling suspicion in the back of your mind that bringing someone a dead mouse was, well, a bit odd – but not at all, they were really into it. They dug the dead mouse, even though it didn't do much except decay. They had lingered so long and hard over the "so" word that your mouse had been a triumph of imagination over conventionality. 'That Zac guy. People would say he's a bit strange but, you know, he bought me a dead mouse the other day, that's sooooo cool.'

We were tucking into our organic free-range roast chicken with trimmings when her mum said to me,

'Zac, don't you need to phone your parents?'

I shook my head. That's the problem with dead parents. They can be even more annoying than live parents. And they don't give lifts on demand. Ari glanced up at me shyly and smiled. Her mother looked up at her quizzically.

'Zac doesn't have any parents,' said Ari, just like that, as if it were her news, hers to say, but I was glad she did, as I found it always made people awkward. Her mother was predictably thrown. 'Oh, I'm sorry to hear that Zac. Would you like some more salad?' The salad had come to the rescue. I was saved by a lettuce leaf. It's amazing how useful random greenery can be. There was an awkward pause. You just had to love her. She was so polite, not going to press me or anything. I spoke up. 'A car crash, I'm afraid, killed instantly. I don't remember them, not much anyway. I live with my uncle Paul. He's all right. He's a policeman. Yes, I would like some more salad please.'

Anne looked down at me, smiled. 'I'm so sorry to hear that,' she said quietly, loading up my plate with mangetout and couscous. Strangely she didn't linger over the "so" word. I warmed to her for that. Great stuff, mangetout, says it all really. If you've got a mouth full of mangetout you don't have to explain the awkwardness of life. I shovelled it in, a middle-class mangetout junkie.

'Being a policeman's not so bad,' I replied.

Ari smirked. Anne turned away, a little flustered. It was a stupid joke. I hadn't meant for Ari's mother to feel uncomfortable. 'I'm sorry,' I said, 'I just don't talk about it, you know, and that's enough salad, thanks.' I didn't know if I could eat all the mangetout after all.

Peters looked at me strangely. It was the first time he had really spoken. 'What's your surname Zac?'

'Zuzak,' I said, adding, 'do you know my uncle?'

He hesitated. 'No, I thought maybe, but no, sorry, wrong person.'

Now here's the thing. He knew I was lying. I could tell he knew, a certain smile on his lips. The way when he spoke, the sentence just tailed off. Also, he knew that he had clocked me, but he was too nice to pursue it. But here's the weird thing, deep down I knew he was lying too. I wish I'd listened to my inner sleuth, but I didn't. It would have saved me a lot of heart break. I just wanted to believe him.

We changed the subject, rapidly, and had a good lunch. It was nice to sit round with a real family, talking, being natural, and eating food that hadn't been fried, battered, processed, made up of several dubious animal bits or deep frozen for several months. It was food that had been allowed for a short time to run up and down the fields breathing in fresh air. Shame it had preferred to stay in-doors and play Warhammer games. I could feel the vitamins and minerals racing up and down my body. I was sorry that I'd lied to Ari's mother but what could I have said? That my parents were junkies who over-dosed on crack cocaine, heroin, crystal-meth, whatever dumb drug had finally flipped them over to the tunnel with the bright light at the end? It wasn't a calling card, was it? Pedigree counts. They would hardly have liked their precious daughter mixing with the son of junkies, would they? It might be contagious. Who knows what the boy would have access to?

I suppose it could have been worse, my parents could have served time in banking. They could have been journalists or worked in publishing.

The truth was, Paul was obsessed with the dangers of drugs. He'd seen too many corpses in his work to not take drugs seriously. I once come home with a tin of baccy, mixed with a little weed, and a packet of roll-ups. He went ballistic. He confiscated it which was a bit difficult because it was Matt's.

When I told Matt what had happened, he beat me up but that was ok, fair enough. I was a bit bruised, but we were friends straight afterwards. He didn't hold it against me, simply never offered me his stack again. I guess that was a good result.

I keep my illustrious parents out of the picture, and it wasn't true, if you want to know, that I didn't remember them, because I did. I was like, you know, young enough. I saw it all. I remembered everything. It's a movie that plays over and over again in my head. Walking into the kitchen as a child, seeing my mum slumped over the kitchen floor, vomit, and piss everywhere.

When we finished our lunch Peter's asked me if I played cricket. I shook my head. 'No.'

'Well, that's a shame.'

I shrugged my shoulders. Cricket was a game played in some other universe to mine.

'Do want to learn? My daughters aren't interested, and Josh prefers to row.'

Of course, Josh preferred to row. Josh was a few years younger than me, and never said anything to anyone, just sat upstairs in his bedroom playing with his x-box. I won't mention him again. It's not that I didn't like Josh. It's just that he kept himself to himself, which I realise now was a smart strategy. I was never introduced to Ari's younger sister. She rarely said a word, and just stared at me as if I was a not from this planet. I suppose she was right.

'Sure,' I heard myself saying.

He set up nets at the far end of his garden with three stumps. Then he showed me how to bowl and bat. It was quite straightforward really. Apart from hitting the ball with the bat. I never got that bit, and why was a cricket ball so hard? If ever a cricket ball gets batted to me, I'm not going to catch. I'm just going to run in the opposite direction.

One Saturday Peters took me to a one-day Test Match at Lords, England v Australia. It was great, apart from, you know, the result.

'You should come more often.'

'No money for that.'

'Money is just a state of mind,' said Peters.

He bought me a pint which was, I guess, not allowed but no-one seemed to mind. His friends were fun too, a bit old-school but good fun. They didn't patronise me. They all seemed to have known each other for a long time. There was a chap there called Richard. I didn't take to him at first, bit pompous, lived in Bath, red trousers, something high up in the MOD, knew a lot about nuclear submarines. Then Peters told me that Richards liked dressing up as a Roman gladiator at the weekend. Apparently, it wasn't a security issue. Everyone was like that in Bath. It would have been considered odd if he hadn't.

After that I mowed Peters' lawn every Sunday, even when he they didn't need it doing. Ari thought it was because I liked her, wanted to see her but really it was just to be with a proper family. I liked them. Also, they gave me lunch, as I had planned that first night in the garage. The money was useful too. I don't know what I was saving up for, apart from the house that is, but it was good to have cash. I discovered that later in life about myself: that having money took away the need to acquire stuff. It was only when I was broke that I became acquisitive. Don't get me wrong, I did like Ari, but she wasn't the main attraction.

8

Lilly was Ari's grandmother. I mentioned here earlier. I don't know how old she was. Pretty ancient, slightly bent over but always neat as a pin, sharp as one too. She used to bring me a glass of cold orange juice after I'd mowed the back lawn. Proper orange juice with bits in it, not the orange drink that Paul bought in cartons that sat in dark corners of the fridge, brooding about the time it had once been an orange. We understood each other, Lilly and I, the moment we met. She knew why I was there. I couldn't hide anything from her. She could read directly into my soul. One afternoon, I joined her on the patio. She was wearing pearls and a twinset.

'You've done a good job there Zac.'

'Thanks.'

She lit up a roll-up, offered me one. I declined, not too sure what was in it.

'My son disapproves.'

'So do I.'

She lit up, took drag. 'We've all got our vices.'

I started to wind up the lawnmower cable. 'Not me. I'm perfect.'

'You're a liar, that's what you are.'

'It's true, I am but then if I say I am I'm actually saying I'm not, you thrown by that? Want me to go?'

'Of course not sweetie. We're all liars, you're just not especially good about it: but don't worry, give it time. It takes practise. I find it endearing. Sometimes a lie has more truth in it than the real facts. Tell me about your parents.'

She'd gone straight to the heart of the issue. I don't know why, perhaps because I knew it was pointless hiding things from her, but I told her everything: about my parent's parties, the places I used to hide, the day I found my mum curled up on the floor, her body stone-cold, stinking of faeces and piss. How my dad just drew into himself then went walk-about: the police, the social services, the whole fucking mess. Good that my uncle was a copper, saved me from a lot of grief that did.

She listened quietly. 'Leave all that behind you Zac.'

'I will. Don't worry about it.'

She told me about her life too, not straight away but little by little. I sensed there was a lot she wasn't telling me. We'd be there nattering for hours. She'd been married a few times. Peters was her second husband's son. They'd lead a quiet life but a boring one, stockbroker land, comfortable but dull. She'd travelled a bit too, mainly New York to see the galleries, the Guggenheim, Museum of Modern Art. I envied her that. It was a place I'd always wanted to go to.

One afternoon she asked me, a propos of nothing, lowering her voice, if I'd heard of "Singular Dynamic." It was a name I was never going to forget.

'Nope, what are they? A Boy Band?'

'They're an investment fund, unit trusts.'

'Peters invests in them?'

'I'm afraid he does.'

She seemed hesitant, nervous. I'd not seen her like that before. Normally she was so self-assured.

'Why afraid?'

She shoved a few pieces of papers into my hand. I glanced at them, some sort of a bank statement.

'I've lived a long time. There's an old saying "When something appears too good to be true, you know what? It is".'

I frowned. 'I don't get you.'

'I don't know why I'm telling you this. You're just a kid.'

'You mean the numbers are wrong?'

'I think so, yes.'

'Deliberately wrong?'

I looked at the papers in my hand, massive sums but they

meant nothing to me.

'I hadn't realised that he was doing this well.'

She leaned back in her garden chair. 'My son's not as smart as he makes out. It was his father who made the money. You know that?'

'Sort of guessed it really. Peters, he's a great guy but I can't imagine him making money. Not anymore. I did at first.'

'You like him don't you?'

'It would be hard not to.'

'Help him. He's in too deep for his own good.'

'But what can I do?'

'You're good with numbers, at least that's what my granddaughter tells me. Just check it out for me, that's all. See if it stacks up.'

'Ari's as good as I am at maths, if not better. Why not ask her?'

'Because she can't know. I don't what her involved.'

'Ok', I folded up the papers and put them in the back of my jean's pocket with a confidence that I didn't have. I had no idea what she was talking about.

The following Saturday I went to the town library to find out everything I could about Singular Dynamic. I knew the staff there quite well. I liked to do my homework in the study area. I went on-line, read a few articles, saw their site. It seemed very successful, had been expanding quickly for the past five years. If I had any money I'd have put it in. There was nothing for Lilly to worry about.

Then I went back to my studies, GCSE exams in in a few weeks' time. They'd dominated my life for a long time. It was important to me. There had been so much rubbish in my life that statistically I was supposed to do badly. It was an almost forgone conclusion; except I knew the opposite. Doing well was a way of spitting in the eye of the fate that the socio-economists had planned out for me.

9

When I'd learned some chemistry formula for a test the next day, I drifted over to the financial reference section and stumbled on a book out about a 1920s criminal called Charles Ponzi. What he did was nothing new but somehow the practise just got stuck with his name. I skim read the book quickly, fascinated, and then it happened, a lifetime's interest in crime was born. I saw my future panning out in front of me. Here was something I could relate to. My Vocation.

It was easy. You set up a fund offering big returns from a new investment scheme, say, high tech start-ups, pharmaceuticals, technology. Investors pile in. Then you pay high returns to the initial investors out of the money from the fresh investors. As long as new punters keep coming into the scheme you're ok, but as soon as they start asking for their money back then you're stuffed because there is no fund, no money-making scheme, nothing. All you've been doing is returning their money to them and paying yourself a very large management fee – keeping the whole cash cycle turning. Everyone thinks they're rich. They want to believe the lies you are telling them, and the bigger the lies the more willing all the professional firms, the lawyers, the auditors, and the bankers are to prop you up. They want to part of the feeding frenzy and it's in their interests to support the Big Fat Lie. The aim is that the BFL becomes so big it can't be challenged.

It seemed quite a good idea, cool really. The only problem being is that it was illegal. This legal or illegal business is such an inconvenience. Lots of people have lost lots of money to these scams. Lives ruined. Retirements impoverished. People taking their own lives. No such thing as a victimless crime. I was hooked. Was SD just another Ponzi? I had no idea or no way of finding out whether it was a BFL or not.

I looked at the documents Lilly had given me. The fund had been set up 5 years ago and had grown exponentially by at least 20% a year. Under the term of his holdings Mr Peters was doing very well but, of course, he'd never received any money back. It was locked into a capital scheme. He would lose 2% of his holding if he withdrew. It didn't really matter if he never received a penny, on paper he looked rich. He could show the holdings to his bankers, borrow against it, acquire even more assets. Everyone was happy. Why spoil the party?

He'd invested £12M in the fund, right at the beginning when it was launched, which had grown to £30M. I did the maths and then the maths again. The library was about to shut. Then I came across the trust directors, the main one being Sam Cutter. I scribbled the name down on a scrap of paper and scuttled out of the library before I was thrown out with all the other homeless bums, schoolies and OAPS with no-where better to go. Maybe one day I should invite them all to my garage? We could read newspapers and cough loudly all day long.

When I got back to the flat Paul was awake. He'd cooked a stir fry. It was just about the only thing he knew to cook but it looked pretty good. I wolfed it down, not enquiring too closely what was in it, but I suspected the remains of last night's Chinese takeaway played some part in his creation, and maybe even the Indian take away from the night before. Paul had a multi-cultural approach to cooking.

'What you been up to then?' he asked, piling more rice on my plate.

'Just revision, that's all.'

'You out tonight?'

I knew what the question meant, a sly little first sortie into the real issue. It meant that he wanted me out so Sharon could come round. I shook my head innocently. 'No, do a bit more revision, quiet night in. Mr Thorpe said not to go out, stay-in, that's best. Plenty of time for going out when the exams are over.'

Paul nodded his head sagely. 'Want a beer?'

'Yeah, why not.' I could tell he was desperate. I guess middle-aged men are all desperate, not so much as young men though.

'It's good to study', he said, 'but it's also good to, you know, relax. Life work balance, that's what it's all about.'

I took a swig of the beer from the bottle. 'Yup you're absolutely right but there are times – as I'm sure you know really well- when "work life balance" has to go out of the window, but just now it's work. For me the main thing is, you know, the work.' I was almost enjoying myself, 'Work. Work. Work. That's the way forward for me.'

Paul swung round and faced me on his chair. 'Ok Zac stop peeing about. How much do you want?' A man will do anything to spend time with his girlfriend. Well, he will do at first before the roses wilt and the chocolates grow stale.

I reached in my pocket and handed him the piece of paper with Sam Cutter's name on it.

'I want a name check done.'

He looked at the paper. 'You mad?'

I grinned. 'When she's coming round?'

'In about half an hour, eat up.'

'You'll do it then?'

'What's this man to you?' he asked quietly.

'I have a friend. He's invested heavily with him. I just want to make sure the guy's on the line.'

'So now you're a financial investigator?'

'You'll do it? It's just to help a friend, that's all.'

'Who is this friend?'

'I'd rather not say.'

He sighed exasperated. 'Ok, I'll make it look routine, say I was searching for a name some low-life mentioned. Don't ask me ever again though. I could lose my job through this.'

I learned something then. Everyone has their weak point, when morality goes out of the window, and for my uncle it was Sharon. I couldn't see the attraction myself, but for her he was willing to lose everything, and to be honest I suppose I was the same about Peters and his family. I stood up, the plate empty, and stretched out my hand like Oliver Twist in the poor house.

'What's that for?' he asked. This was again a similar routine.

'Cinema. I'll be back about 11'

'Make it midnight'

'Done'

He gave me a twenty-pound note. I headed for the garage where I'd spend the rest of the evening. We both knew I hadn't been to the cinema in years, but I had a large amount of cash stacked away in my secret tin.

Later that week Paul grabbed me just before I went to school. 'I ran that report you asked for.'

'And?'

He thrust a print-out in my hand. 'You'd better read it.'

Written in police code with abbreviations and guarded language the report was brief but condemning. Sam Cutter was known in Europe and America as a possible fraudster, but nothing stuck. He'd been arrested a few times in New York and London, but the charges had been dropped. In his early days, before he graduated into the big league, he had run bucket shops, boiler rooms selling junk bonds or shares that no-one wanted at high prices. Somehow he'd always just avoided the law, and if anyone in the press tried to write about him his lawyers would close in like hungry sharks after a blood-soaked turtle.

'Can I keep this?'

'You messing with me?' Paul took the report back and set fire to it with his lighter, throwing the flaming paper in the sink where it burned to cinders. 'I don't want any hard evidence of my running off checks for non-police business. That could cost me my job, you know that?' he reminded me, angry at himself.

'Yeah, I'm sorry. I shouldn't have asked you.'

Paul's voice softened, 'this friend of yours, is he in deep?'

'I think so.'

There it was, a problem, all thirty million of them, and being sixteen I reckoned I could help, the dangerous optimism of the young and naïve. There's another old saying, "no good deed goes unpunished." I wish I'd known it then.

A few days later I was with Peters. He wanted to do some bowling practise. When we'd finished we sat exhausted on the lawn. There was an awkward silence. Peters could tell I wanted to say something, 'What is it kid? You got a crush on my daughter? You could do much better you know?'

I laughed, 'no, I was talking to Lilly the other day.'

'Oh, I see, always dangerous. I've seen you two together, both just friends I hope? Nothing romantic? I think you're a bit old for her.'

I took a deep breath, 'she told me about Singular Dynamic.'

'So now you're discussing my personal affairs. You want me to invest for you?'

I shook my head, 'no, it's just,' I hesitated, 'Cutter has a bad reputation. You know that? Why invest in him?'

'So now you're an investment guru? Any more tips?' Peters stood up, clearly irritated, 'let me give you a tip. Stick to your GCSE's' He walked off. I didn't raise the issue again.

10

It was simple really. I went into Peters' study, pretending to be searching for him, calling his name. The address book was on the table. I guessed that he wouldn't be very bright about where he kept the codes, and I was right. They were written out neatly in the back in his best black ink handwriting.

I whipped out my mobile, snapped the last few pages then strolled out of the room, my heart beating wildly. It didn't take me long, just a few minutes but long enough for time to feel like slow motion. At the same time, I felt a real rush. It was like scoring a goal. Addictive.

Then I mowed the lawn just like normal as if nothing had happened, another day, only it wasn't a normal day. It was another change-day, after which nothing could be the same again. I'd crossed a line into a whole new country.

I've discovered that sometimes things happened like that. We do something, meet someone, make a decision, sometimes even something really simple but we don't realise that it's set up a chain of actions from which our lives will never be the same again. It takes bravery to acknowledge these moments, if we knew about them, or thought about them with any real depth perhaps we'd never do anything. I mowed the lawn in stripes and raked up the cuttings, dropping them in the compost the way Lilly liked.

I caught Ari looking at me through her bedroom window, but she didn't come out to say "hallo" I think I embarrassed her. Most things seemed to embarrass Ari, even herself. When I'd finished mowing the lawn, Lilly bought me an iced orange juice as she always did, our little ceremony. I took a sip and she looked at me, one inquisitive eyebrow raised. She knew that I'd been up to something. I told her everything I knew about SD and Sam Cutter. I was proud of myself. The report was comprehensive.

When I finished we paused, watched a blackbird singing loudly on the willow tree at the end of their garden. I didn't tell her about my little foray into Peter's study.

'So how do you know all that then love?' she asked.

'My uncle, of course. He really is a policeman.'

'I thought that was just one of your stories.'

I shook my head. 'All the best lies have an element of truth in them.'

'You're a one. You're learning fast.'

'What we going to do about it then?' I asked but in a funny way I already knew. I'd already worked it out. It was in my head.

She knew that too. She took my hand and squeezed it. 'We'll think about that, shall we? Just the two of us. Best not talk about it to anyone. Especially Peters, you understand?'

'Ok. Where is he?'

'Playing golf with his buddies this morning, I think." She stood up and pottered inside. I cleared the garden tools away.

I was about to leave when I bumped into Ari. She had decided to risk leaving the sanctuary of her bedroom, the safety of the duvet. She was looking as lovely as ever, a little lock of blond hair sticking to her forehead. Without thinking I leaned forward and gently eased it back. She seemed surprised, blushed.

'Zac, I need your help. Moon-face has given me an impossible maths problem.'

It was weird of her to ask because Ari, though I hate to admit it, is probably even better at maths than me. We went into her dining room. Her papers were spread out on the table. We sat close together and worked through it. Her mum, Anne, came in with orange juice and garibaldi biscuits. Eventually I realised what Mrs Moon had done.

'Ari, this problem, there is no solution.'

Ari looked up at me, chewing the end of her pencil, which to be honest I found distracting. 'What do you mean "no solution"?

'I mean it's a trick question. She's trying to teach us something.'

'What's that?'

'That sometimes there is no answer, only a question.'

She put down her pencil, 'what are we going to do now?'

We wrote out all the attempts we had made, the dead ends, the workings, the different ways into the problem. It was kind of fun if you enjoy puzzles. When we had finished there was an awkward silence.

'I suppose I'd better leave.'

'Stay a bit Zac, there's something puzzling me.' She turned a shade of light pink.

I shifted uncomfortably, 'what's that?'

'Well, why have you never made a move on me? You've had plenty of chances. I'm curious.'

'Er … I … um'

'You're not gay, are you?' she added quickly, 'I'm cool with that, only it's not me is it?'

'What do you mean?' I was genuinely confused by now.

'You don't find me, you know, unattractive? I should have got a complex by now through your lack of interest. I should be anorexic, have self-loathing suicidal thoughts. You seem more interested in my grandmother than me.'

'Ari,' it was my turn to go red, 'yes, of course, you're gorgeous, you're more than that. You're uber-scrumptious.' What on earth was I saying? I sounded like a complete idiot.

'I don't make you feel suicidal do I?'

She screamed with laugher, 'only when you try to dance at the school disco.'

'Well, that's a relief.'

I wanted to ask her what was wrong with my dancing but thought better of it. This was a conversion about her. Then she leaned forward and asked me, 'do you want to kiss me?'

Hard as it is to believe, girls don't normally ask me that kind of thing. I said, 'ok'. I tried to sound casual, but it came out as a little too eager, and a pitch too high. I moved my face towards her.

She moved rapidly away, 'I didn't say you could kiss me, only if you wanted to.'

'I'm sorry. You mean in an abstract theoretical way rather than in a practical hands-on approach?'

'I didn't say anything about hands-on. I suppose a little empirical testing is valid,' she said, grabbing me by the neck.

We kissed. Can I just say that again? We kissed. It was awkward. Her eyes were staring at the door in case anyone walked in and disturbed us. Our lips met and her tongue just sort of popped in and explored all my molars and fillings like one of those Mars rover explorers. We heard footsteps and pulled away.

Her mum walked in. 'Brought you some Ben and Jerrys, hope you'll like cookie dough.'

I thanked her, gasping for breath. The woman was clearly two steps ahead of me, and one step ahead of her daughter. She left the room and I stared at the ice cream with a psychotic hatred. Ari simply picked up a spoon and tucked in. Thinking about it afterwards I realised that she had planned it because her top brace was missing. I was no match for these women. It was a lesson I should have taken greater note of.

'That was nice', I said.

'Which? Me or the cookie dough?' She picked up her pencil and doodled on the paper in front of her, 'it was ok' she said.

'Just ok?'

'Yes, not like kissing Gary. He's a really good kisser.'

I stood up indignantly, 'you've kissed Gary?'

'Oh, don't be silly. Everyone's kissed Gary'

I sat down, 'I've not.'

'I should hope not. Oh, you are gay, aren't you?'

'No, I assure you it would be no problem if I were, but I'm not. At least I don't think so. Mind you, I have watched Top Gun more than is healthy for a boy my age.'

'But you agree the kiss was just ok?'

I conceded the point. The truth was I had limited experience in the whole snogging scene. For me it was "bloody fantastic" but I acted cool.

'I know', she declared, 'you can be my Gay Friend. Every girl should have a Gay Friend and you can be mine.'

'But', I protested, 'I'm not gay.'

She looked at me, exasperated, 'for someone who's so clever you can be really stupid, can't you? Look, we're friends and we want to hang around together, yes?'

'Yes?'

'Well, we can't do that unless you're my boyfriend because everyone will assume that you are my boyfriend and then I'll never get a proper boyfriend. Doesn't that make sense? I'm sorry but I don't want to be seen with you. It would ruin my image. But if you were my Gay Friend then I can still get a proper boyfriend, and we can still hang around together.'

I had to admit that there was something logical about it. Although it did sound alarmingly like John Nash's Game Theory, and he won the Nobel Prize for that. Perhaps Ari was a genius after all? Alternatively, may be it was just because she was teenage girl with all the insecurity and ruthlessness they all have. Basically, let's face it they are all geniuses.

'There is only one problem with your little theory' I muttered.

'What's that?'

'I won't be able to get a Proper Girlfriend.'

Ari giggled and tossed her hair back, 'but silly, there's absolutely no chance of that is there? Let's be realistic now.'

I had to admit. She had a point. I shrugged my shoulders and left that day with the newly established dubious status as Ari's Gay Best Friend Forever, a GBFF, life is so complicated, give me something simple like Fermat's Last Theorem anytime. Maybe it was time for my gay phase, just get it over and done with.

11

You might want to skip this chapter if you don't like technical stuff but, frankly, it's not really complicated. The best crimes are the simplest. I want to explain to you how I did it, how I stole thirty million pounds, but please don't try this at home. It could get you in to trouble. It will get you into trouble.

I waited until Paul was doing a late-night shift. He thought I was in the garage revising for my exams. I should have been, but I just had to get this out of my system. I couldn't concentrate. I took £50 from my savings in the tin and took a bus to the Tube. I bought an oyster card with cash. Nobody could trace my trips. I wore my hoodie up. I'd bought it from a charity shop. Nobody had seen me in it before. I think I looked cool. I resisted clawing at my crutch. If you're going to commit a crime there's no point in looking badly dressed. Then I travelled across London, keeping my head down. There are thousands of cameras on the underground. I just tried to look anonymous, nondescript which was not difficult, my normal state really.

I stopped a few tube stations away from where I was going and walked the distance to the Interstellar Café, a naff name. It's just a grungy internet place, somewhere in the West End, the seedier part of Soho. They also arranged international wire payments, currency conversion that sort of thing, and probably a lot more besides. I hoped Paul wasn't outside in an unmarked vehicle.

Most of the cubicles were full, but I paid my money for an hour and found a place in the middle of a crowd, better to merge in. It was night-time the guy managing the desk was reading a science-fiction paperback. He looked as if he hadn't slept in days, probably addicted to computer games, like some of my mates, or maybe studying to be an actuary. He didn't get a peep at me, and the security camera looked like a fake.

I sat down, took a deep breath, and created a few e-mail accounts, you know the type that are free for the first three months. If you don't use them they get scratched. I thought they might come in useful, a warm-up exercise. I've got a good memory for numbers and passwords, so I had all of Peter's numbers in my head, the ones I'd snapped in the back of his diary. I'd deleted them from my mobile and bought a new memory card just in case, having broken and thrown away the old one. I'd seem people do that in the movies, so I did the same. I guess I'm a bit paranoid, but I just wanted to reduce any trail as much as I could. Anyway, it felt dangerous.

I logged on to Peters' bank account and opened a new on-line account in his name, using his NIC social security number and pin. The closer I kept things to real-life the better. It was easy because it was his existing bank. Also, I'd helped Paul set up his on-line account. I knew what I was doing. Paul was rubbish over the internet, a real digital dinosaur, a digitosaurus.

The new on-line account opened instantly but stated, as I knew it would, that a pin and card reader for that specific account would be sent to me within the next three to five days by registered post. I made a mental note to myself to keep an eye out for it, look around his office. He tended not to open his mail unless he really had to. It just piled up in the hall, along with the offers for pizza or dog massage, until something had to be done about it.

Then I logged on to Peter's e-mail account and had a good look around. There was nothing there of interest. An automated e-mail popped up, declaring that a new on-line bank account had been set up. I forwarded it to one of my fake addresses then set up a rule on the system that any e-mails from that address should be automatically forwarded to my fake address. It was an instruction deep inside options. It would never occur to Peter to look there. Then I deleted the e-mail on his computer and went in to the delete box and deleted my delete.

There was nothing much in his e-mail, mostly unopened junk, but there was one folder that had all his SD investment e-mails with attachments. I opened the latest and pulled down a pdf statement. By all accounts he was doing well. For a moment I almost bottled. I thought to myself what am I doing? I could ruin this man's life, never mind my own, but then I looked at the figures carefully, capital growth returns every year of 20% - 30%, even during the difficult years when I knew, from research, that similar trusts had struggled to break-even or even do that. It was ridiculous, especially during a recession years.

How could Peters have fallen for it? I suppose he was just one of many. The current value was £30M and he had put in £12M. It was all an increase in book value, nothing had been taken out in dividends.

I took a deep breath and placed a series of sell orders on the account. I wouldn't take it all, just most of it. I sold an even proportion of each category of holdings, global managed trusts, corporate bonds, Far East funds, something called Alternative Instruments: probably no-one really knew what they meant or cared to. Only a few knew that the money he had invested had probably gone up someone's nose. I suppose that's what they mean by Alternative Instruments.

I gave the new bank account and all in all I sold just under £30 million. Again, an e-mail popped up from SDT investments. I repeated the action as before, setting up a forward rule but this time to a different e-mail account. Then I deleted and deleted the deletes as usual. None of this was waterproof. It would fool a man like Peters, but any proper computer security analyst would pick it up, but Peter was not the sort to worry about things like that.

Then I leaned back on my chair. I'd only used half my credit time. I logged out of all the accounts and then went into the cache to delete the history of the accounts I had visited. I stayed for another thirty minutes playing a dumb internet game to make it look as if I was a genuine punter. I didn't erase the cache for that one. I was proud of myself. I had slain a dozen zombies and discovered the diamond in the wizard's lair. My credit ran out, I slipped out of Interstellar Café, never to darken its doors again, the whole experience had been simple, stella really.

On the way home I took a different tube journey, and this time I used a ticket that I had bought with cash from a machine. I also took off the hoodie I'd been wearing, threw it away which was a shame because I thought I looked good in it and put on a beanie hat I'd been carrying. I would be hard for cameras to track me.

Paul would have been proud, well perhaps not, furious and astounded I would say. But to my reckoning, if I was right about SD and Cutter – and I was pretty sure I was - I had just saved Peter at least £30 million. Cool. I could only hope Sam Cutter was a crook. I just didn't know.

Ari's family are all really disorganised. Their post lies unopened on a table in the hall, along with assorted free newspapers, schoolbooks, and the occasional dead mouse, but not the one I'd given them. Filtering through it to find the registered letter, pin and card reader was not difficult. There was also a debit card which I'd not been expecting, so I took that as well. It was so easy. Peter didn't suspect a thing, but Lily did. She saw the smile in my eyes but said nothing, and I saw the twinkle in her eye.

Then, weirdly, nothing happened. The world did not blow up. The money sat in the account. Only I knew it was there and had access to it, but I couldn't worry about that because something far more important had happened. It didn't really take me by surprise but for some reason in all the excitement I had forgotten about that terrible rite of passage that afflicts us all and brings even the mighty low. I am course not referring to my GCSEs but to the prom afterwards. Exams came and went, and I performed as expected. It was all less exciting than it had been built up to be. The only worthwhile thing about it was that I found I could misbehave badly, and Paul just let it go. It obviously dismissed it all as pre-exam nerves and didn't want to create waves. I think I could have carried out a major cyber crime and got away with it. Oh yes, I had done that.

12

I prepared for my Second Proper Snog (SPS) with military preci-sion, mouthwash, floss, the lot. The post-GCSE party had been ar-ranged at Jake's house. Surely, I had to have some luck? I had to get-off with someone, or what was the point of living?

I decided that the kitchen would be forbidden to me. It was a place for losers. Unfortunately, I had not reckoned with my repu-tation as Ari's GBFF. Lawrie, one of the school's knuckle-dragsters, greeted me at the door, 'gay boy, welcome.'

I smiled weakly, 'Don't you know it's not cool to make homophobic comments?'

He looked at me, confused by the multi-syllabic word. I smiled patted him on the shoulder good naturedly and headed straight for the kitchen, where Jake, the rugby captain, was pour-ing punch down his throat. He offered me a glass.

'What's in it?' I said cautiously.

'Dunno, whisky, gin, vodka, beer, bit of cider, some stuff I found in the back of my mom's laundry basket. Whatever we could find really.'

'I'll stick to my beer.'

'Sensible mate,' then he paused, looked at me rather strangely and said quietly 'I thought that was really brave of you, you know, coming out like that, more than I could do.'

'What are you saying Jake?'

He paused, 'well I too am a member of The Rainbow Nation.'

'Oh, I see, you're South African?'

And that was it really, my evening was over. I had to listen to Jake's torments, as a fellow traveller so to speak.

'As the school rugby captain, I should, you know, really be beating you up. Part of the job description. At least tormenting you daily. Trouble is I just can't do that. I just feel love towards everyone, even you.'

'That's very kind of you Jake.'

It was particularly humiliating because he kept on assuring me that I wasn't his type. Was I anyone's type? I couldn't tell him I wasn't gay, well probably not. It would have humiliated him, then he might have beaten me up. Ari came passed and blew me a kiss. I frowned at her, and she gave me the finger, charming. Soon the music grew louder and some of my friends got over excited, dancing in a weird way, part South Korean hip-hop part Care-in-the-Community. The cool kids weren't there. They'd gone off to Newquay or the Reading festival to smoke elephant poo, catch pneumonia, have piss thrown at them and set fire to their tents. Fun.

One of Ari's friends, Serena, came up to me, 'Ari asked me if you've Seen Her Guitar Case.' She said each word syllable by syllable and looked at me pointedly. I put on a confused expression and asked her to repeat herself, which really seemed to irritate her. I shouted to her over the music, 'but she doesn't play the guitar'.

'Don't be an arse Zac. She wants to go home.'

Jake looked at me a bit weirdly, I thought that he was so off his head that he didn't really know what was going on. The contents of his mom's laundry basket had got to him. He leaned forward confidentially, 'that's code for "please get me out of here". I gave him a kiss on the cheek and left. It was time to leave the party. I had flossed in vain, but it is better to have flossed in vain than never having flossed at all, a triumph for dental hygiene over teenage ardour.

Gary was coming on to Ari and she clearly didn't like it. He had her trapped in a corner. I walked up to him and tapped him gently on the shoulder. He turned round and glared at me, then grinned and asked if I wanted to meet Molly. I nodded. What a loser.

'Yeah, Molly here then?' I said.

He winked, 'I'll see you in the back garden.'

Business was business and he slipped off.

I looked at Ari, 'guess we've got five minutes before he realises I'm not coming.'

She picked up her handbag, 'let's go.'

As we left I spotted someone emptying the goldfish bowl into the punch. That would surely improve the taste. No sure how the goldfish felt about it.

We ran the first few hundred yards to be well clear of the house.

Ari turned round to me, out of breath, laughing, 'who is Molly?'

'You don't want to know'

She frowned, 'don't tell me. I'm sure she's really nice,' then she stormed off walking in front. I thought about explaining to her that Molly was a little pill you took to feel happy but decided that I was too tired, so I followed behind her at a discrete distance just to make sure she was ok.

When we arrived outside her house, she turned round and beckoned me to her.

She looked up at me, 'let's forget Molly.'

'Ok.'

Her beautiful face was lit up in the moonlight, 'isn't this where you kiss me romantically?'

'Yes, but we're not friends like that. Have you forgotten? I'm your GBFF.'

'Look, my little sister's staring at us in the top window. If you don't kiss me I'll never live it down.'

'If it keeps your sister happy, I'm prepared to make the sacrifice.'

I kissed her. It was better this time, but it didn't last too long. After a few minutes, she pushed me away 'You can go back to Molly now.'

'That's fine. Feel free to use me for sex anytime.'

13

Peters sat hunched up in his office chair. I walked up to him tentatively, 'you ok?'

He looked up and raised a glass of whisky at me, 'you want one Zac?'

'I don't drink, not spirits. Well not on a school day.'

I looked at a newspaper on his desk. He had circled a small article in the business news section. The headline was: "Sam Cutter arrested as latest Ponzi scheme collapses; thousands lose their life savings."

It was strange that during that whole exam phase I'd thought nothing of my little cyber adventure. Then it all flooded back to me. He took a sip, 'you know kid, I really am bust. It would have been better if I'd put the money under the bed.'

'I'm sorry. How much did you lose?' I asked innocently.'

He shrugged his shoulders, 'alot.'

'No really?'

'Well, I only invested … a small amount. It was my wife's inheritance. I feel so bad. We'll have to sell the house now. Get somewhere a lot smaller.'

I didn't know why he was lying to me. He probably didn't want to admit the scale of his stupidity.

'Well, it's not as if I didn't warn you.' I regretted saying the words as soon as they came out of my mouth.

He looked up sharply, 'you did. I should have listened to you, but you know what? I don't normally take investment advice from sixteen-year-olds, even if they are a maths genius.'

'I wish I were.'

He leaned back on his chair and stared into mid space, 'so how did you know about Cutter then?'

'My uncle. He's a police officer. I told you. But don't tell anyone he looked at the records. He could get fired for that.'

'That's true is it? I thought it was just one of your stories.'

I felt myself turning red, 'what do you mean "one of your stories".

He paused and looked away, 'I know about your parents Zac. Your dad was a good friend of mine.'

I didn't know what to say. I just felt angry, 'so you knew him?'

'Yes I knew him. As I said, we were mates. I tried to steer him off the hard stuff but there was nothing any of us could do.'

'Tell me about him.'

He paused, 'I will do, I'm sorry I didn't say anything before. I didn't want to upset you. Not before your exams.'

It was my turn to hesitate, 'I need to show you something.'

'Can this be later? I'm a bit preoccupied. Can't you see that?'

I shook my head, 'no, sorry. I really need you to see this now, just a few moments.'

He raised an eyebrow. I gently took the laptop from his desk and typed in the URL for the bank. Then I logged in to the new account. I took a deep breath and swivelled the screen round so he could see it. He looked down, confused.

'What is this Zac?

'It's a bank account.'

'I can see that. Whose account is it?'

I said very quietly, 'tt's yours.'

He looked up at me, 'you are taking the mick mate?'

The account showed a balance of just over a £28 million with a little interest on top.

He took the laptop from me and looked over the account, 'it's in my name.'

I nodded, 'yes, it's your money, like I said.'

'What have you been doing Zac?'

I crossed to the end of the room near the door and sat down, 'I knew Cutter was a crook, just like I told you, so as a bit of insurance I sold your STD stock, well most of it, and moved it in to a secret account.' I grinned, proud of myself.

He started shaking, 'Zac mate, you're a blooming genius.'

'Thanks.'

He knocked back his whisky, 'how did you do it?'

I told him. I don't know why. I suppose I just wanted to get it off my chest. Maybe it was just boasting. I told him about looking at the back of his diary, about redirecting his e-mails, taking his post. It was all so easy, but what I didn't notice was his body language. His shoulders grew tauter and his face long. When I'd finished there was a long uneasy silence in the room. He snapped the laptop shut.

'Zac. You've saved this family. You really have. You've saved us from financial ruin ... but do you know what you've done?'

'It was in your name. It was all above board. The money left the account months ago. They'll never trace it.'

'You've thought of everything.' His voice was sad and low. I knew something was wrong.

'I'm sorry if I deceived you Mr Peters. I was concerned.'

'Deceived? What you did, I don't know what to say Zac, on the one hand I'll be grateful to you for the rest of my life, on the other ... well, you crossed a line, didn't you? And that's the problem.'

'I'm sorry I saved you millions' I said icily.

'You're just like your dad. He could never respect boundaries either, always going a step too far, never content just to walk away from situations. It's what killed your mother in the end.'

I got up shaking, 'you bastard.'

He walked up towards me, trying to put his hand on my shoulder, 'Zac, how can I trust you in future?'

'Don't you touch me.'

'Zac, I didn't mean to upset you mate, I'm just a bit shaken up myself.'

I shouted at him, 'you should never have said those things. What do you know? What do you f***ing know about anything?'

I ran out of the door into the hall. Mrs Peters emerged from the kitchen and called out my name. I opened the front door, grabbed my bike, and pedalled furiously away. As I left the drive I glanced behind me. Lilly was at the window and our eyes met. She had known about me from the first, but she was all right was Lilly.

When I got back to the flat Paul was occupied. I could tell. I slipped into the garage, turned on the heater and collapsed on to my make-shift sofa bed. I lay on my back and stared at the ceiling. It was funny in a way. I could revenge myself on Peters because only I had the codes, and he could hardly explain to the bank that he'd just forgotten them. I'd let him sweat for a while. By now the bank site would have timed him out anyway, I chuckled to myself then lay on my side and started counting again:0, 1, 1, 2, 3, 5, 8, 13, 21, 34, 55, 89, 144,233,377,610 … and then I fell asleep.

14

I avoided Ari at school. I wasn't welcome at her home anymore, so she could just FO. They could all just FO. Why did everything end up so screwed for me? I couldn't focus on school.

Kept of thinking of Mum, I'd only caught sight of her that once, before someone scooped me up and lead me away: a picture of her just lying there on the floor kept on running through my head, her hand stretched out, the stench of piss. I tried to force it out of my mind, but it bubbled back every time. I don't know why now. I felt like bad all the time.

I avoided everyone, sat in the library, staring at the book in front of me. I was on my own again. Rest of the time, I just slept or tried to.

Once Ari passed me in a corridor. She was so beautiful I could barely look at her. She'd grazed her knee. She looked sideways at me.

'You avoiding me?'

'Guess I'm not your GBFF anymore.'

'My Dad's been asking after you. The lawn's looking wild.'

I stared at my shoes.

'Bromance over?'

'Something like that.'

'Honest, you're worse than girls in my class. What was it about?'

'Can't say.'

'What happened to your knee?'

'Can't say', then as an afterthought, 'don't look at my legs.'

We only had another week at school then the summer holidays, eleven weeks before the sixth form. The teachers weren't really bothered what we did. Most of my friends were going away. I could lay low during that time. Maybe try and get a job.

She looked annoyed.

'See you in year 12 then?'

I nodded. 'yea, see you. Well, let's hope so, results permitting.'

She walked passed me, flipped her hair.

'You'll do ok Zac. Just get your butt round to my house or I'll have to do the gardening.'

She went into her class, the end of year school play. I wasn't in it. Drama's not my thing. My acting career peaked at being the back end of a camel in a year six nativity play. I'd made a complete arse of myself.

It was prom tomorrow, all Laura Ashley and no knickers. I wasn't going, not my thing either, too American. The girls loved it, excuse to buy a dress or three, but I couldn't ask Paul for more money, and I didn't have the shoes to match my frock. Besides I'd spent all my cash trying to save Peters. At least I'd succeeded in that. Not that he really appreciated it. If it wasn't for me he'd be selling the Big Issue.

The night of the prom I wheedled some cash out of Paul to go to the cinema. He wanted a bit of privacy again. As I took the money it occurred to me that perhaps he didn't really care about me at all. It really upset that he had a love life, and I don't. I'm supposed to be the rampant teenager, instead I'm exiled to the garage with a pair of socks for comfort, not matching ones either.

He knew as well as I did that the money just went into my pocket and I've never been to the cinema. He's never even pretended to believe me and ask me what I'd seen or who had been in it, which was a shame because I did detailed research for my cover story. Sometimes when I watch films on tv these days I kind of know the plot because I'd meant to have seen the film when it came out. It was convenient to believe a lie. That's why I like numbers, lies just don't work in maths. Numbers lead to the truth and from that there's no escape, no convenient lie. But sometimes it helps us all to believe a lie, it's a comfort. I was just an inconvenience to Paul, no point in lying about it.

I went to the corner shop and bought myself a bottle of cider and a large packet of crisps, living on the edge, living the dream. I slipped back to the school and from a hidden vantage watched a few of the girls climbing into a stretch limbo. It was all so kind of American. It made me ill.

I went back to the garage and amused myself by working through a textbook on arithmetic sequences. I wanted to master index notation so I could follow the Cauchy sequence. Then I curled up in my sleeping bag and dreamed of her for a while before I went to sleep. I remember that clearly because when I woke up she was looking down at me and I was embarrassed. I thought I was asleep and maybe she knew. Only it wasn't Ari it was her grandmother Lilly. She looked a bit like Ari, but I swear I'd never dreamed of her, not in that way. I propped myself up on my elbows.

'What are you doing here?'

Lilly picked up my notebook on index notation, flicked through it, took a good look around.

'This where you live?'

'What are you doing here?'

'Get up. Get dressed. We'll go somewhere for breakfast. Ari around? You hiding her?'

There was something about the tone of her voice. It wasn't the time for a quip.

'No,' I said, quietly, 'she ok?'

'I don't know.'

Lilly slipped out, waited for me. Soon as I left the garage she grabbed my hand.

'Was Ari with you last night?'

'Only in my dreams'

'Be straight with me Zac. Where is she? She didn't come home.'

'I swear, she's not here'

'When did you last see her?'

'She was at prom.'

'Were you there?'

'Of course not'

'Then how do you know Zac?'

'I saw her right She got into a limo with those harpies she hangs around with. I saw her. She was wearing a long green dress, silk, with a curl on the collar, black shiny shoes, a slight heel, and she had her hair cut back, quite short, a silver Alice band. She had a gold bag, with a twinned cord. I'm not sure, I couldn't see too good. She may have been wearing pearls. Did you lend them to her?'

Lilly sighed, 'that was her. I lent her the pearls. What about her friends? Who was she with?'

'I dunno. I didn't look at her friends. Only Ari'

I realised what I'd said. There was an embarrassing pause.

Lilly smiled, 'it's like that is it Zac?'

I looked away, 'I guess it is.'

We went to a café nearby. I had tomato sauce with my chips. Lilly sipped a cup of tea.

'Peters told me about what you did'

'I was only trying to help.'

She patted me on the hand in that kindly way she had, 'I knew I could rely on you.' At last, someone who appreciated me.

'Look, she's probably crashed out at a friend's house.'

'Let's hope so, my dear.'

'If you're worried I can ask my uncle. He's police. He'll get her looked for.'

Lilly dried the corner of her mouth with her napkin and folded it on the table, smoothing it out with her hands. I watched her.

'No police,' she said.

The cafe seemed quiet all of a sudden.

'Why?'

'It's Peters. He's been arrested.'

'Done something wrong?'

'No, that crook Cutters. Seems like he knows him. When you sold the shares, it started a chain reaction. The whole scheme collapsed. Everybody tried to get their money out. Only thing, Zac, as you so shrewdly worked out, there wasn't any money. The FBI moved in on Cutters, had him under house arrest. Only Cutters disappeared. Then a man appeared at the house, started threatening Peters unless he coughed up the money he'd made, said the children were in danger.'

'Shit.'

'Only Peters couldn't pay him a farthing'

'Why not?' I asked but the moment the words were out of my mouth I knew the answer. Yup, I'd really screwed up. I had the passwords, the codes to the accounts. They were in my head and nowhere else. I had caused this. It was me. What had I done?'

'I can give him the codes.'

'You can't do that.'

'Why not Lilly? Oh, Lilly I'm so sorry.'

'My son, not the brightest of boys, he flew to New York to try to reason with Cutter but as soon as he got off the plane, the FBI arrested him. They think he and Cutter are in some sort of alliance.'

'I'll have to go out there, tell them.'

'No, at least Peters is safe in custody. It's Ari I'm worried about.'

'She knew about this?'

Lilly shook her head.

'You think they may have her?'

Lilly looked at me, 'maybe. But if we go to the police, Cutter will send her back in pieces.'

'But we don't know, for sure, do we Lilly? She could be at a friend's house.'

'You got a mobile?' she asked.

I gave her the number.

'I'll text you when I hear.'

She bustled out of the café. I ate the final chip and went home. Paul was asleep, snoring his head off like a diver grappling with an aqualung, so I had a shower, dug up some less dirty clothes from the laundry pile. Then after that everything happened very quickly. I got a text from Lilly.

'They've got her. Cutter wants his money.'

'I can give you the codes?'
'No, Zac. Sorry, Cutter says you have to see him.'
'Where is he?'
'New York'

I looked at those two words for a while. What had I done? This family had only ever shown kindness to me and instead I'd really damaged them. I was so screwed. I went to the bathroom, ran cold water over my wrists, splashed water over my face, sank to the floor. I had to think. Ten minutes later I was waking Sleeping Beauty from his slumber.

'What is it Zac?'

15

He got up, made himself a coffee. Thing about Paul, he couldn't think straight without caffeine in his blood stream first thing in the morning. Now the thing about lies, the best lies is that you have to be close to the truth, but so fundamentally different that it misleads, then little by little the truth and the lie converge into each other, like one of Cauchy's sequences until eventually the two are so indistinguishable there is nothing of any substance left. I told Paul about Cutter.

'You know the guy you ran the report on?'

Paul groaned, 'don't remind me.'

'Turned out he's a big-time crook. He's after Ari's family.'

'She's the skirt you like?' he said, grinning

'It's serious. The family suggest I lay low for a while.' I told him what I knew, just omitted the bit about the money laundering and cyber-crime. Thought it best to be discrete about that bit.

Paul stood up, 'f*ck's sake Zac. What have you got in to?

I shrugged my shoulders, 'sorry. How was I to know.'

'It's best if you go, slip away quietly for a while', said Paul.

'I've not got any plans for the summer.'

'How about youth hostelling? It's a good cover. I'll say I don't know where you are, probably somewhere in Scotland "he won't answer his mobile, typical teenager."'

Then Paul pushed his credit card across the table, 'take this.' He told me the code.

I picked it up, 'thanks … look, I'm grateful …'

Paul leaned forward and punched me on the shoulder, 'don't be stupid.' Perhaps he did care after all?

I went into my bedroom, packed a few things in my ruck sac, just enough for hand luggage. I knew what I had to do. Paul would be the last to hear of it. I left the flat quickly. Paul thrust some money into my hand, a few hundred. I put it in my back pocket. He gave me a bear hug and I slipped away. I went into the garage and took a few things, my passport included.

I went to Kings Cross railway station and bought a ticket for Waverly Station, Edinburgh. I used Paul's card to throw off the trail should anyone come looking for me.

Then I took the Piccadilly line to Heathrow, terminal four. I bought a ticket using Peter's card. I felt a little guilty about taking his money, but I knew he would understand. It was for him after all. I took the shuttle to Paris-Charles de Gaulle.

Something I've not explained. At school and everywhere I'm known as Zac Zuzak but that was just for convenience. It was Paul's surname, my mother's younger brother. Legally, I was named Zac Crossland, my father's name but I never used it, not until now that is, but it was the name in my passport. Again, if anybody tried to find me they would never look under the name of Crossland not to begin with.

There was no flight to New York to begin with. I had to wait for five hours for a seat with Air France. My heart was in my mouth when I bought my ticket, but the card went through, under the reasons for travelling I put 'checking out American Universities, undergraduate courses'. I was the right age.

The lady at the booking desk pointed to a screen, 'any seating preference monsieur?'

I shrugged my shoulders, 'not really, as long as the girl next to me is pretty'. Of course, I didn't really say that. I just thought it, but the lady must have been a mind-reader. Or perhaps I did say it out loud without thinking? The stress was getting to me. She smiled, 'bien sŭr, of course monsieur, this is France.'

I'd read a book where a man had pretended he was afraid of flying so he could ask the girl on the seat next to him to hold his hand during take-off. A bit creepy I know.

When the plane started to fill up I found myself in a window seat at the front. A large elderly man squeezed himself in beside me. He really should have bought two seats. There was no ignoring him, 'Hi.' He grunted and spilt further into the seat. I decided that my fear of flying was cured. I wasn't going to try and hold his hand. The booking desk lady had a great sense of humour.

I enjoyed the flight. I'm one of those strange creatures who likes aircraft food, all those little cartons, wraps, plastic knives and forks and things. I don't mind that eating it is statistically more dangerous than flying. At one point I thought about going to the loo and giving myself one. Matt would have been impressed, but I guess it wouldn't really have counted as joining the mile-high club. My application would have been rejected. No white stones for me.

Soon as I got to New York I caught a taxi to Cutter's office. What else could I do? It was the only thing I could think of. The office block was concrete and glass with a marble atrium. There was no water feature though, which was a shame. I walked up to the reception where two ladies wearing identical black suits sat directing the stream of visitors to their respective firms.

'I'd like to see Sam Cutter.'

'Are you delivering?'

I guess I didn't look like an international banker, which must be a compliment.

'Yep,' I lied.

'We'll sign for it here.'

'No sorry, it has to be signed for by him.'

She looked at me severely. 'there's no Sam Cutter here.'

'I'll take it to the Singular Dynamic office then.'

'Ok, please yourself, third floor, take the lift, be quick. Only there's no-one there.' The lady beside her sniggered.

The office had a secure keypad in the door, so I rang the bell.

After a few moments a man opened the door and stared at me. He was bald, heavily built and wore a shirt a size too small, with a name tag on his lapel, 'Henry Gull'.

'Hallo Henry, I'm here for Sam Cutter'

'You the delivery boy? Just give me the package. I'll sign for it.'

'No, I got to see him. It's in my head.'

'You're not a courier are you?'

'No.'

'Where you from kid? You sound like a Brit to me.'

'Just tell him I'm a friend of Peters.'

'You'd better come in then.'

I walked nervously into the office. The door clicked behind me. The place was full of police. I'd expected to see sharp suited executives and friendly staff wearing pastel-coloured cardigans with knitted ties. Instead, there were just a lot of what looked like detectives. Not sure I liked that. Now that I had got here I wanted to make sure I could leave whenever I wanted to. They were going through all the filing cabinets, desks, and computer records. There were boxes everywhere stuffed with files. It looked even worse than the garage.

'We're the FBI kid,' he showed me to a room, 'someone will be with you soon. We'll hear what you got to say then.'

My plan wasn't working too well. I didn't want to end up arrested like Peters, especially not by the FBI. They're not as cuddly as our lot. I began to panic. I had to get to get out of there quickly. This would never lead me to Sam Cutter. They'd put me on the first plane home if I was lucky. Peters would end up in an American prison charged with conspiring with Cutter to defraud.

They'd be looking for someone to blame. Peters would be the perfect person to pin it on. I could see that they were all too busy to bother with me, but I wouldn't be allowed to go unless I made a distraction of some kind. I sat staring at the wall for a while, trying to control my breathing and considering my options. Then I hit upon a plan. It wasn't a good one but at least it gave me a chance.

There was a fire alarm button in the room. My finger hesitated over it for a few moments then I pushed it. The alarm went on, red lights, sirens, the lot. I have to admit that it was kind of satisfying.

A recorded voice bellowed over the office intercom. 'Fire alarm. This is not a drill. Please leave the building and gather at your evacuation point outside in your muster groups. Do not take the lift. Do not take the lift.' Then the message repeated itself.

The man with the undersized shirt came back into the room, 'you'd best follow me.'

I walked behind him down the stairs but soon we were surrounded by others, all desperate to escape. I slipped back and mingled in the crowd. By the time we were out via the fire exits the man was far ahead of me. I joined a different muster group then when no-one was looking, slipped quietly away. Easy.

16

I caught the subway back to a hotel bedroom. It felt safe in there. I had no real idea what I was doing. Only if I met Cutter, what could I say to him? I thought about having a drink as there was a fridge in the corner of my room. There was beer, wine, spirits of all kinds but I just had a diet coke. I'd broken enough laws that day. I wondered how soon it would take for the FBI to work out who I was.

I stayed in my room until about seven pm then felt hungry. I showered and got changed. I was just about to leave when there was a knock on my door. I opened it carefully. Outside was the woman who had been on reception. She was chewing gum and looked angry. Whoops.

'You want to come in?' I asked her, in all innocence.

'What do you think I am, a hooker?'

I took a step backwards, 'sorry, just you know, being polite.'

'Oh yeah, you're English, forgot that. You're taught to be polite. Sam wants to see you. You hungry?'

I nodded. We took the lift down.

'How did you find me?'

'I followed you, you were easy to tail. English secret service not teach you anything?'

I grinned, 'I'm not MI6.'

'Then what are you honey?'

I don't know why. Perhaps it was just the jet lag, but I decided to tell her the truth.

'I'm in school.'

'Columbia?'

'Er no'

'Cornell? Fordham? Don't keep me guessing honey.'

'Well, you won't have heard of it. I think you call it High

School here,' I said lamely.

She stopped, uttered an expletive then tilted her head back in laughter, 'you're in high school?

'I hope you've got something good for Sam. He's a busy man, you know that?'

We left the hotel and she flagged down a yellow taxi which took us to a Chinese restaurant in Manhattan, Fuby Roos. She took me to a discrete table tucked away under the staircase, said "wait here" and disappeared. I sat there for a while wondering whether the enigmatic Sam Cutter would turn up.

Eventually a young waitress appeared with a trolley of dishes. She arranged them on the table.

'You like.'

'Er, yes .. but I didn't order this.'

'You not Mr Larsson?'

I shook my head and then a voice behind her said, 'I'm Mr Larsson.'

I stood up. The man in front of me was Sam Cutter, short, jet-black hair, in his forties, just like his mug shot on the police report I'd got Paul to print off. We shook hands. The waitress went to serve another table.

'Why the false name?' I asked.

He gave me a don't-be-stupid-look and sat down.

'Let me tell you something Zac, a little "tradecraft" if you like. Never give your real identity, not when you're in our business.'

I didn't like the mention of "our business" but just grinned. Perhaps I was in that business now, or at least on a youth apprenticeship scheme.

He thought for a few seconds then added, 'always pay in cash and keep moving. That's my advice.' Then he gestured to the food in front of us, 'you like Chinese?'

'I do, and thanks for the advice.'

'New York has the best Chinese restaurants in the world and this in the best one in New York.'

'I'm flattered. I don't eat out that often,' I thought of the chip shop I went to when Paul locked me out.

'Do I call you Mr Larsson or Mr Cutter?'

'Sam will do.'

We piled the food on our plates, steaming rice, noodles and bamboo shoots, duck, and delicate delicious parcels of food.

'I'm hungry. I've been in America all day and not eaten anything.'

'This is your first Breakfast in America?'

'Yeah I think it is.'

We both started laughing. Truth was, I could not help but like him. Why is it I always like the wrong people?

He turned serious, 'why you're here Zac? You're a bit young for a career in organised crime. By the way, you're not wired?'

I stood up, 'oh no, look nothing on me. Besides I had to give the FBI the slip this morning.'

He leaned back on his chair and laughed, 'I heard about that. Not a great start to your first day in the Big Apple, but I like your style. Tell me where you are staying.'

'Your girlfriend knows. She followed me there.'

'Is that how she described herself?'

I shook my head.

'Make sure you check out tomorrow, real early and don't take the hotel taxi, ok? Walk a few blocks and then hail a cab. Never stay anywhere longer than a couple of nights.'

'And pay by cash.'

'You're a fast learner. But why you here? You know Peters?'

I took a deep breath, 'it's about Peters.'

'He sent you?'

'No … but I thought I'd make a deal.' Then I explained. I told him it was me that took the money. Only I had the codes. Peters couldn't do a thing.

'You some kind of computer nerd?

I nodded. Another lie but I had to draw him in somehow. Truth was that apart from my ICT course at school I knew nothing much about computers, just how to turn them on, that kind of thing. I'd even mastered how to turn them off. It was the stuff in the middle that confused me. I continued, 'you must stop asserting that Peters was in it with you.'

'He's the only one who made any money. Looks a little odd don't you think.'

'You know as well as I do it'll be years before he's found not guilty, not unless there's proof. It'll bankrupt him and .....'

'And is this my problem?'

'I can get you the money. I know the account codes and the passwords. I just need to see you say that Peters had nothing to do with your operation.'

Cutter took a sip of wine, 'you're a cool customer kid. You and me, we're quite alike really.'

'No we're not, you're the bad guy. I'm the goodie.'

Cutter laughed, 'Bad guy, good guy. You still believe in that? They all merge in to one. You think the FBI will believe me? You think they care about you? What are you doing this for? You like Peters and his family. What's his daughter called? Arianne? You like her?'

I nodded.

'You think I'm not driven by love either. Love for my children. My

family,' said Cutter.

'Love of money?'

He shrugged, 'and that too. Sure. This is the United States of America. It's practically written into the Constitution.'

His phone rang. He picked it up and made a few comments then showed me the screen, 'it's for you.'

I looked at the screen. It was Ari. She was crying. 'Zac ... Zac, is that really you?'

'Ari, where are you? Are you ok?'

'Zac, they're holding me. I'm so sorry. I just thought I'd come out here. Talk to them ... but they're holding me.'

The cell phone went blank as the call was cut. Cutter leaned over and snapped it shut. I looked down at my food, no longer hungry, the world draining away.

'She's got nothing to do with this,' I shouted at him. People in the restaurant looked up.

'Whoa kid, keep your voice down. Want to attract attention to yourself. I guess that means you don't want desert. I can recommend the Song Goa.'

'Release her.'

'Release the codes.'

I thought frantically. It was hard to keep cool when every inch of my body yearned to lean over and punch him. Shove his face into his duck blood and vermicelli soup, or whatever it was.

'Not until Ari is free'

He smoothed down his napkin on the plate, 'let's do an exchange.'

'Ok but it has to be somewhere public.'

'How about the Smithsonian?'

I thought for a while but that did not seem a good idea. I needed somewhere super safe.

'Westpoint.'

He looked at me sharply, 'sorry?'

'Westpoint military academy. It's about 60 miles from here.

'I know where it is kid ... but.'

'Not even you would do anything stupid there,' I said.

'How do you know I won't cut off her fingers? That I haven't got a group outside ready to pick you up.'

'Because you're a financial criminal Mr Cutter. You're not a thug.'

He got up, 'tomorrow at 10 pm then, make sure you're on the guided tour. We'll do the exchange on the bus.' He left.

I stared at the wall. Diners were eating their diners, enjoying each other's company. The pretty waitress came up to me and smiled. I grinned back, hoping that I had charmed her somehow.

She uttered the immortal words, 'you want bill Mister?'

Of course, why had I assumed that Cutter was paying, silly of me. I nodded, 'I want bill, thank you.'

I paid quickly, shocked by the size of it, which would have paid for my school dinners for at least a few terms. My finger would have broken. I asked for a doggy bag, no point in wasting it but she looked insulted, a misunderstanding I guess. I left a generous tip and caught a taxi back to the hotel. Thank goodness for Paul's credit card. Not the normal type of Chinese takeaway he bought. It would be hard to explain, but then what wouldn't?

17

I decided to take Cutter's advice straight away. If I had been found once I could easily be found again. I paid my bill and checked out. The hotel offered to get me a taxi, but I turned them down. It was late by now and by the time I'd walked a few blocks there weren't any of those yellow taxis.

I hung about a bit but there were a couple of guys who walked past me talking loudly. I thought they looked a bit scary, lawyers. I spotted a subway and went deep into the underworld. I'd sleep on the subway that night. I caught a train, put my gear underneath the seat and set off. I changed before the last station to avoid being rounded up with the shady company that gradually filled the carriage and were obviously also trying to find somewhere warm to sleep. I thought about recommending me town library to them. Instead, I took four trains, two difference journeys there and back, about 40 minutes sleep each way, although not a deep sleep. It was too dangerous.

When I emerged back into the daylight it was early morning, but some fast-food cafes were opened. New York never really closes. I had a cup of black coffee and big breakfast, and by big I mean that I would never have to eat again.

I felt exhausted. Only a little sleep last night but at least Cutter had not got to me a second time. I flicked on my mobile. There was a text from Paul asking where I was. I felt a bit guilty. I texted back that I was 'ok, not to worry.' It was a BFL because, of course, I was not OK and there was every reason to worry. I looked around the café, all chrome and red faux leather seats. I could hang out here for an hour or two, read the papers, have yet another coffee. The café had free Wi-Fi. I took out my laptop and logged in to my favourite website on maths, praying that Blue would be there. I sat in the back so I could watch who was coming in. A waitress strolled up to me.

'A black Americano please,' I asked.

'You a Brit? I just love that accent.'

'Does that mean I get my coffee free?'

'Nope'

She came back a few minutes later, put the coffee on the table. There was a large chocolate cookie, 'that is for free,' she said, with a lovely smile. You've got to love America.

'Thank you.' I said, in my poshest English voice.

I waited for the coffee to cool down, took a few sips. I could feel the caffeine pumping around my heart, up to my arms and brain. It was waking me up slowly from the metro journey that never ended. I picked up a paper that someone had left and turned to the sports pages, not really understanding anything of it. What is a foul fly ball when it's at home? Is this the US equivalent of a silly short leg?

Two men walked into the café. They looked like Mormon missionaries, tidy short hair, identical, smart dark grey suits. Apart from that I couldn't describe them to you. It's as if they had been custom-made for anonymity. They ordered coffee, so not Mormons then. I could hear them chatting to each other in a dull tone. Without a word they both got up and sat on my table, one opposite, the other beside me. I pretended not to notice, just studied the baseball scores as if I cared or understood anything. I could hear one of them stirring the teaspoon in his cup. Head bent over; I lifted my eyes from the paper.

The one with the teaspoon was staring at me.

'You want the paper?' I asked, pushed it over to him, 'makes no sense to me anyway.'

'We're looking for someone,' said teaspoon boy.

'Can I help?'

'Maybe'

I got up to leave but teaspoon boy's friend was blocking my way. He dropped two sugar cubes into his cup. I sat down again.

'We're looking for this kid, about your age, from London,

calls himself Zac – ring any bells?'

I shook my head, 'no sir, can't say I know anyone like that but I'll keep my eyes open.'

Sugar cube boy leaned over, 'thing is we reckon it's you.'

I rolled my eyes, 'me?'

The waitress glanced in my direction. I could see she was nervous. I got up again.

'Sit down', said Teaspoon man, 'don't jerk us around.'

He flashed his card at me. I think it said FBI but to be honest I had no way of telling whether it was real or it had just come out of a Christmas cracker, but in the circumstances I sat down anyway, seemed the most sensible course of action. Teaspoon man took the lead, 'what are you doing here kid?'

'Honest answer?'

He nodded.

'I have absolutely no idea.'

The waitress came up to me, 'these men bothering you honey?'

'Yes. They are,' I said.

One of them flashed his card at her.

'I'd like you both to leave. This is just a kid here.'

They both stood up politely, 'yes, ma'am.'

I was astonished. I had not realised how powerful waitresses are in the USA, or how polite the FBI.

Teaspoon boy handed me his card, 'we're watching you, boy. You're in deeper than you know, understand that? We want to keep you safe. You phone when you're ready but make it quick. We can't hold off for long.'

I took the card. He smiled. I sensed he was ok, but I couldn't risk Ari by getting them in the picture.

18

I paid the bill then went to Times Square and took the Short Line bus to Westpoint. It took about an hour and a half to get there. I got off outside the West Point visitor's centre. It was about 12.30 so I took a guide bus round the campus. I had to show my ID which was a risk but there was no way round it. The security demanded it. The bus sat there for a while, churning away, as more and more people got on, most of them elderly, but no sign of Cutter or Ari.

Then just as it was about to leave, I saw them both get on. I waved to Ari. She grimaced back at me. Cutter beamed and waved. He seemed so friendly, just like a dad out with his kids. He made his way towards me and squeezed my shoulder, 'good to see you son.'

'You too,' I said and passed him an envelope with all the codes inside it.

Ari sat next to me. She slipped her hand in to mine. It was trembling.

'You got the codes?' she whispered in my ear. I nodded, 'just given them to Cutter', and I offered her a piece of gum. Ari never chewed gum. She took it and smiled, 'thanks for being here.'

'I'm sorry', I said, 'If I'd just let things be neither of us would need to be here.' And I really meant it, this would be the last night I messed about in anyone's financial affairs.

Soon the bus pulled up outside the museum. We piled off the bus and went in, pretending to admire the artefacts.

'You didn't think it was going to be that easy?' said Cutter smirking.

'I've given you the codes.'

He looked impatient, 'well I'm not going to try them out here am I? Who knows what you've planned?'

Ari was looking with great enthusiasm at a WWII Liberator pistol. I never known she'd had such an interest in small arms.

'She stays here. I'll go with you.'

'OK,' said Cutter.

'You don't make the decisions Zac,' said Ari, 'I'm coming with you.'

Cutter was looking at us, amused.

'Please, trust me on this.'

Ari scowled then strode away, turning to look at me briefly as she went to the next exhibit room. As Cutter and I left, I caught the eye of the cadet standing casually by the information centre. I knew it was Blue.

Cutter and I rode the bus back to the car park by the visitor centre. We strolled past a tank to the car park. We could have been father and son. Cutter drove a grey mustang. Despite myself I couldn't help admiring it.

'If you steal enough money like me, kid, one day you too may own a car like this,' quipped Cutter.

I rolled my eyes, 'so how many people did you rob of their life savings then?'

'People made an investment. Just not a good one. They did ok. I gave them a dream for a short while. A dream is worth something. It would have worked too but for your little escapade, causing a stampede.'

I leaned back on the leather seat as the mustang roared on to the R218 towards the Highland Falls. Then after that I lost the route.

'I've done the maths. These schemes always fall at the end.'

He lit a cigarette, 'forgot you're a maths whizz kid. Sums were never my strong point at high school.'

'Why do all this for just a few million dollars Sam? There's no point to it.'

'Got to pay my defence lawyer somehow, besides … it's a question of justice. I have to revenge myself somehow.'

'That's what this is all about, revenge?'

'You how old son? What do you know about anything? Bet you've never even had a pussy. Don't give me no sermon.'

'I did have a cat once, for a short time. But it had fleas. Had to go.'

Cutter glanced at me, not sure I was joking.

I remained silent and glanced nervously at the wing mirrors hoping to see a car behind us, but there was nothing. We stopped talking after Cutter's outbreak. After a few hours we took a remote side road up a mountainside, then turned sharply on to a dirt track. As we drove up higher the landscape became more desolate. The car stopped at a house hidden by huge douglas firs and red cedars. We got out. A freezing cold wind whipped past us, cutting through our clothes.

'Home sweet home', murmured Cutter as we scuttled in to shelter. Just as we stumbled in through the front door I saw a fresh leaf curled up on the doorstep, but it wasn't from any of the trees around here, a red maple. Perhaps it had come off our shoes.

The building was a handsome chalet in the style of Frank Lloyd Wright, half suspended over a ravine. The view from the lounge was panoramic, looking out over the mountainside towards the wilderness. It was getting dark now. I wondered where Ari was. What was she doing? I suddenly wanted to be with her, just to see her face, hear her laughter.

'You hungry?'

'Yup.'

I wondered if this was to be my last meal, and if Cutter would kill me after I'd helped him with the codes. Nobody had followed us. I was alone.

Cutter searched through his fridge. It seemed empty except for some stale cheese. Eventually he found a packet of crisps and a few tins of fizzy drink.

'This will have to do,' he said, then walked to the next room. Despite my fear I gobbled the crisps down. They were good. I couldn't tell then flavour though, either stale chicken or stale salt and vinegar. Around the room there were photographs of a younger Cutter with his wife and two children having a barbecue somewhere grinning at the camera.

He appeared back in the room with a laptop, 'we used to come here. Back in the days when I had a wife and family.'

I said nothing.

'Ok just do the transfer then I'll release you kid.'

'You mean drive me back to Westpoint?'

He shook his head, 'no, no just open the front door that's all. What do you think I am? This isn't a taxi service. You said yourself I'm not killer. You'll just have to chance it out there. Not too many wild bears at this time of year. That's fair ain't it? I'm giving you a chance.'

'There really bears?'

'How would I know? Do I look the outdoor type?'

He flipped open the laptop and switched it on. Using the codes I gave him, we logged in to the bank account quite easily. Peters had not known of it. There was £25M in the account plus interest. Then we tried to make a transfer but it wouldn't work. Cutter looked up at me,

'Nice try kid?'

'Yeah well. You didn't think I would give you the transfer code, did you?'

'I got to your girlfriend once before. I can do so again.'

I shrugged, 'I'll need some paper.'

He handed me a notebook and a pencil. I scribbled down a code: cut246303234

'How come you remember that?'

'It's easy, first three letters of your name then the next is just the first six numbers of the eban sequence'

'The what? You're confusing me.'

'The eban sequence, pretty cool, simple, kids' stuff. First number is 2 because in the spelling two there's no 'e', then the next number is four … and so forth.'

'I see, that's it.'

'Nearly. I scribbled out the website address, and his customer code.'

He picked it up, 'that all?'

'You'll need this too, your doohicky'. I gave him the pass calculator.

'Oh yeah, of course. What's the pin?'

I wrote it down, 'all this is what you need. The money's yours. You win. Can I go home now please mister?'

He smiled, 'I always win. You need to know that. But I like you. Maybe one day you can work for me.'

'The sorcerer's apprentice?'

He grinned, 'something like that. Anyway the money on its way now. It'll snake through Vanuatu, the Cayman Islands, Panama, so many accounts nobody will be able to trace it. Not even you Zac.'

It was a shame Cutter was the baddie. I couldn't help but like him. Just then the doorbell rang. He froze. Took out a pistol from his back pocket. I backed away. He signalled me to get down on the floor. I dropped down. Cutter opened the door cautiously and peered out in the dark. There was no-one there. Suddenly the lights went out, but it wasn't pitch black as it was early nightfall and there was a still grey light that filled the rooms. Beautiful, life hung still for a second.

19

Just then I heard a tremendous bang. A man was swinging outside the window. He'd tried to smash through the patio window, but it was reinforced glass. He just hung there helplessly.

'Friend of yours?'

'Just hanging about'

Blue looked at me, lifted a mobile in his hand and pressed a few buttons. I thought that the glass would break in to a million slivers, but nothing happened.

Cutter slide open the windows, 'reinforced glass, sport, you ok?'

We cut the swing ropes and lowered Blue gently to the floor, 'I think I may have broken my nose.'

He took off his helmet.

'Let me look,' Cutter gently inspected his face, 'badly bruised I'm afraid. You should really have used the front door. Its customary, you know and polite.'

'I was hoping to take you by surprise, sir,' muttered Blue.

'Well, you sure did that.' Cutter pottered into the kitchen and came back with a wet dripping tea towel, 'I've put some ice in here, hold it up to your face'

'Thanks'

Blue looked at me. He rolled his eyes, 'Good to meet in person.'

'Sam's a fraudster not a gangster,' I said, not quite knowing why I was defending him.

Then Cutter surprised us both by pulling out his gun again. We stepped back nervously. He pulled the trigger, a flame shot out and he lit two candles on the mantelpiece before him, 'we need some light. Getting dark here.'

Blue started to giggle nervously. So did I. Suddenly neither of us could stop laughing.

Cutter watched us both, amused. Then he asked softly, 'when do the grown-ups get here?'

Blue looked at the floor, 'I don't know, sir. Soon, I should imagine.'

'How did you know we were here?'

'Tracker device on your car.'

'You put it there?'

Blue nodded, 'I major in electronics at the Academy.'

Cutter walked back into the kitchen, poured himself a large whisky and dropped a few ice cubes in. He joined us back in the sitting room, an icy blast came through the open patio glass doors. 'I would offer you a drink too, but I don't want to break the law. It's been a pleasure knowing you boys. I'm sure you'll both do well. Plenty of guts and initiative. I hope my sons grow up like you too.'

'I'm sorry,' I said quietly.

Cutter smiled, 'I had a good run.'

Suddenly the room filled with light, and we heard voices. The front door blew up. Cutter, raised an eyebrow, 'why does nobody ring the doorbell these days?'

A woman wearing a black bullet proof vest and carrying a gun ran in to the room, 'on the floor', she shouted, 'arms spread.' Blue and I both complied but Cutter walked slowly on to the patio and leaned back against the railing facing her.

'Get down, sir, or I'll have to shoot. This is your only warning.'

Suddenly I realised what was going to happen. I scramble up, 'no Sam, no.'

But it was too late.

'Work hard play hard boys' were his final words. He tipped himself backwards and fell into the blackness of the night, into the ravine and his death. I stared in disbelief at the space where a few seconds ago he had been standing.

'You stay down son,' this time a different voice, the man from the office who I had shaken off, Gull.

'I didn't think he would do that,' I mumbled

'On the floor, son', this time the woman's voice again.

I lowered myself to the ground and shut my eyes. It had not meant to end like this. I felt someone checking me for arms. Then we were ordered to stand up. The woman put her gun away.

'We lost Cutter out of the window,' she said to the man.

He walked to the patio and stared down over the rail to the ravine below, 'no-one's going to survive that. Let's get these kids looked after.'

A blanket was put over us and we were taken to a waiting truck where a nurse checked us over, 'you're ok, bit of shock that's all. We'll take you somewhere quiet to rest,' he said.

We were driven back to WestPoint. I shook Blue's hand, 'thanks for rescuing me.'

He grinned, 'not much of an entry.'

'The leaf was a good touch, reassuring.'

'I thought you would like that. Catch you online.'

Then he was marched off. I turned to the FBI officer in charge, 'where are they taking him?'

She smiled, 'military jurisdiction. Out of my hands I'm afraid. But don't worry. He contacted us. Put the tracker on your car. Led us to you. I'll put a word in for him'

I learned later that he had had some form of honour trial by the cadets themselves. He had gone off the base without permission, used army equipment and put himself and others unnecessarily in danger. He was found guilty, dropped privileges and, as punishment, ordered on a twenty-mile run with full pack. On the morning of his run every cadet from the trial and his cohort greeted him. They all carried a full pack and ran every mile beside him. That's Westpoint.

20

I spent the night in a room somewhere at Westpoint. I think there may have been a guard outside my room. In the morning, after breakfast, I had a little meeting with the FBI man. We shook hands, 'hallo Henry.'

He looked at me sharply, 'how do you know I'm called Henry?'

'It said so on your name badge. The one in the office. Remember? Henry … Gull.'

He relaxed, 'you drink coffee?'

Another man was with him, 'this is Dr Drake.'

'Dr Drake?'

'He's the shrink, and youth protection as you're technically a minor,' explained Henry.

Drake smiled at me in a creepy kind of way. I nodded back. We sat down and a tape recorder was switched on. Obviously I kept out the bit about my switching the money into a different account. Basically, I said I was a friend of the Peters Family and when this happened, for some dumb reason, I decided to try to sort Cutter out myself. I thought that If I could provide him with some money he would drop his charges against Mr Peters. Unfortunately, his daughter thought the same, so I ended up swapping places with Ari. I'd been a friend of Blue through internet puzzle sites so I chose Westpoint to come to, so that Blue could bring in the FBI and get Cutter arrested for child abduction. I had not meant for Cutter to take his own life.

Gull leaned forward, 'so how did you switch the money Zac?'

There was no point in hiding anything. They obviously knew it already. I told the whole story. Afterwards I was shaking. Gull switched off the tape and led me back to my room. They had provided a few books and newspapers for me to read but I found it difficult to focus on them. I was desperate for TV or PlayStation.

'What's going to happen to me?'

Gull shrugged, 'I don't know, that depends on the authorities.'

I had a miserable sleepless night. I tried the Fibonacci sequence again, but even that didn't work this time. All those arduous rabbits counted for nothing. I suppose the rabbits just weren't comfortable in the USA. The following morning, I ate a light breakfast in my room.

Then Gull arrived, 'let's go for a walk.'

It was a beautiful crisp day, but the wind cut through me. We followed a footpath along the perimeter of the campus.

'You're to be extradited' said Gull.

'What does that mean?'

'It just means that you'll be escorted out of the country, no charges. In many ways, apart from the fire alarm fiasco you've done absolutely nothing wrong. In fact, we owe you a debt of gratitude. You and officer cadet Blue led us to Cutter. He'd slipped bail some weeks ago.'

'Have you retrieved his body yet?'

Gull shook his head, 'no. not yet. They're still searching. We may never find it. The ravine is a long way down, lots of animals could have got him I'm afraid. But our agent saw him jump. One thing that we can be sure of is that he's dead.'

I looked up at the grey green mountains in the distance where Cutter had lived, 'I'm sorry he took his own life. I thought he was ok really.'

Gull said nothing.

'What will happen to me when I get back to the UK?'

'Nothing apparently. Peters has said you acted with his full authority. No-one believes him but what can we do? You've come out of this well Zac.'

I glanced up at him, 'where's Ari?'

'She's nearby. You'll be meeting up with her soon. I believe you're flying back to the UK with her.'

Ari walked into the waiting room shortly I got back. She slipped shyly in and smiled at me, 'you ok?', she said. She seemed older somehow. She was wearing ill-fitting clothes that someone must have lent her.

I nodded, 'and you?'

'Fine.'

We both knew that fine means Fed up, Insecure, Needy and Emotional.

We looked at each other for a few moments then I walked up to her put my arms around her and gave her a big hug. She stiffened at first then relaxed and hugged me back. I looked down at her face and kissed her. Our mouths melted together, and this was really our first kiss, not the other two that we'd had before. Those had just been pretend-kisses. Suddenly we heard voices and pulled hurriedly away, both of us blushing.

Peters walked into the room with Mrs Peters, Anne.

'Mummy', Ari rushed up to her mother and burst into tears.

They were crying. Peters shook my hand formally, 'thanks Zac, thanks for everything, most of all looking after Ari. I'd had no idea she would go off like that.'

I looked up at him warily, 'sure.' The old friendship had gone. He was now just being formal with me, and I felt like crying.

Later that afternoon we took off from JFK International Airport direct to Heathrow. Peters had booked us first-class tickets. He was obviously feeling flush. As the plane took off I took Ari's hand in mine.

Paul met me at the airport. Sharon was with him. He gave me a bear hug, 'glad you're ok. Look can't stay long. I'm on a job in Paddington. Just got the morning.'

'That's fine.'

I said my farewells to Mr and Mrs Peters and Ari. I wanted to take her in my arms as we left but we just gave each other a polite kiss on the cheek. I looked into her eyes, 'skype me.' She smiled shyly and was led away by her parents.

'We'll be in touch', said Peters as they left, but everyone knew that was just a polite lie. Peters would want to put as much a distance between us as he could. We drove away in silence in Paul's car. I was in the back. Sharon in the front. There was an embarrassed silence.

21

To my surprise we pulled into a little restaurant. Paul looked nervous. We sat next to a window. There was a great view, just a car park. The waitress arrived and gave us our menus. I'd never seen Paul look so nervous before.

'We've got some news for you.'

I looked down at the menu, decided to skip the starter, maybe go for the chicken curry. I knew what he was going to say, of course I did. It was obvious. Sharon stretched out and took his hand in hers, 'we're getting married Zac.'

I'd expected the restaurant to go silent, may be the traffic to stop outside but the world just carried on around me as it normally does. They both looked at me nervously not knowing how I would react. Then something weird happened inside me. I don't know what it was, maybe just jet-leg but I looked at their faces; his, tired with anxiety lines stretched across his forehead; hers, perhaps a little too much makeup, a hard look in her eyes masking a vulnerability that I'd not seen before. I felt a huge wave of love for them both, a sense of compassion I'd never felt before. I put the menu down on the table, closed it and said in my most serious voice, 'I suppose that means we're ordering champagne?'

Paul, relieved, laughed and swung back on his chair. Sharon just looked at me quizzically, unsure how to read me. I leaned forward and kissed her on the cheek, 'congratulations I'm happy for the two of you, really I am.'

'Sorry about the champagne though Zac', said Paul, I'm working today so it's just diet coke all round.'

Then Paul shifted uncomfortably in his chair. I hadn't thought through the consequences.

'I'm afraid there's more Zac.'

'Yeah there's always more.'

He paused and my stomach dropped through the floor. Why had I not seen this coming?

'I can't stay with you anymore?'

Paul nodded, not smiling now, 'I'm sorry. Not in the long term, no.'

'Why?'

'Sharon's got two small ones from a previous marriage.'

'I didn't know,' I looked at Sharon, 'what are their names?'

She took a photograph out of her handbag and handed it to me, 'this is Jason. He's five. This is Brittany. She's seven.'

'They're beautiful.'

'Thanks', she swiftly took the photograph from me swiftly and slipped it back into her handbag.

'So...what's happening to me?' It was a reasonable question but an awkward one.

Paul looked away, avoiding my eye, 'I'm sorry mate.'

'Social services not approve of the garage then?'

'No.'

'Shame.'

'You're disappearance didn't help me much Zac. Didn't strengthen my case. You've no idea of the trouble you caused.'

I grimaced, 'I'm afraid I probably do.'

Paul continued, 'they were going to take you away from me anyway, not much I could say. Especially when I confessed I had no idea where you were.'

'Are we talking foster care?'

Paul shrugged, 'well maybe. There are homes too. You'll be given your own flat at eighteen, that's if you don't go to uni.'

I grinned, 'there's an incentive to do well.'

'I'm doing my best. I'll come and see you mate.'

'Yeah, I know. Don't worry about it.'

He looked up at me, 'just in case you ever wondered, I do worry.'

For a moment I almost believed him. I stared at the menu. I wasn't hungry anymore. Truth was that I wanted to cry but that wouldn't have been a good look. Then Paul leaned forward and said something quietly under his breath, 'there is an alternative.'

'What could that be?'

'You could go away to school?'

'Board you mean.'

'Yep, board.'

I rolled my eyes, 'Hogwarts? You can't afford that.'

'No, I can't', he paused, 'but Mr and Mrs Peters can. They're grateful for what you did for them, whatever it was, don't tell me. I don't want to know.'

'Wait until you see the bill from the Chinese restaurant,' I said.

'Don't worry, I've already seen it. Couldn't you have gone for a fast-food place?'

'I'll explain later.'

'You don't have to,' said Paul.

'You've discussed this school thing with Mr and Mrs Peters?'

'Sure, they know all about me and Sharon'

Of course they did. I was always the last to know about anything.

'What school?' I asked, but the moment I said it I knew what the answer was. It was the same school my dad had been too, where he had met Peters. It was the school known as Malhangers, a very old, endowed school in the west of London, impossible to get in to unless you were related to the Prime minister or someone posh. My father had been expelled, hardly one of their most distinguished alumni. It wasn't going to win me any points.

'They wouldn't have me.'

Paul smiled, 'they've already offered you a place.'

I sat up, 'how did that happen then?'

'Peters is a governor and a good friend of the headmasters, besides your results were excellent.'

'Ok', I was beginning to see how things worked, then it struck me what he'd just said, 'you have my results?' I'd forgotten all about them.

Paul grinned, 'you did ok.'

'Just ok? You've opened it?' I suppose I should have been cross that he had opened my results but in the scheme of things I was in no position to complain to the management.

'Do you want to see? I've got the print-out here.'

'Oh go on then,'

He slipped an envelope into my hand. I tore it open, a string of As with little stars attached to them. My mood was picking up. I didn't have a home and a family. My uncle was sending me away to a school, or I was going into council care but at least I now had a starred A for maths. It was official. I was good at sums. The starred A for PE was equally as important to me, I'd really struggled with that one, not being a natural athlete.

The waiter arrived. We ordered our meal. I only picked at mine. I realised that I wouldn't be seeing Ari again. As if reading my thoughts, Paul said, 'do you like Peter's daughter, now you've got to know her a bit better?'

'She's ok', I said trying to sound cool and nonchalant, but blushing all the same.

'Well,' he said, 'she's going to Malhangers too so at least there'll be someone there you know.'

I wanted to jump up and punch my fist triumphantly in the air, but instead I chewed vigorously on my bread roll and feigned indifference.

'What's her proper name?' asked Paul.

I shrugged, 'can't remember. Is it Arabella?'

Then Paul and Sharon chatted on and on about their plans. I smiled and asked polite questions, but I really wasn't very interested. Truth was, I was tired. All I wanted to do was sleep. My adventures had caught up with me. We drove back in silence. I slept. Paul dropped me off and I went to my room. It was just as I had left it, but I knew that it wasn't going to be my room for long. In fact, nothing was mine, not really. I had nothing, and everything was being taken away from me. I didn't have a 'my' anything. I kicked the door and stupidly it caved it, so I got an old poster from the top of my wardrobe and taped it over the hole so Paul wouldn't notice. I was more shaken up than I'd thought.

The only 'home' I'd ever really had was the garage. I ambled down and let myself in through the back garage door. It was damp and cold in there but pretty much how I'd left it. I switched on the wall heater then plugged in my laptop. Good thing the Wi-Fi worked that far. After checking a few lame e-mails, mostly from my mates about their results, and a lot of junk, I took a peek at Malhangers School.

22

There was something that had been bugging me about it, but I couldn't remember what it was. The website was a little slow then the site came on, the usual crud: 'tradition of outstanding teaching, 'generations of distinguished alumni'. How was I ever going to fit in? Then I saw it and my heart stopped for a second; the school motto *'Laboris Gloria Ludi'* which means, correct me if I'm wrong, *'Work Hard Play Hard'*. It was what Cutter had said just before he threw himself off the balcony into the abyss below, bit too much of a co-incidence that.

He was what, how old? Same age as my Dad, had he lived. Same age as Peters. I went to a chest in the corner of the garage. I'd not been into it for years, but it contained a few things that belonged to my Dad, stuff that Paul couldn't bring himself to throw away. I dug up a year photograph, taken just before he'd been thrown out. They were all wearing cricket whites, very public school for those days.

My dad was beaming out of the photograph, creepy thing was, apart from his long eighties' haircut, he looked just like I do now. I almost choked up thinking about him, how his life had panned out. I scanned the photo into my laptop and magnified it. There were two other boys that looked familiar in the top row. Of course, it was Peters and Cutters, looking very young, fresh-faced. It all suddenly made sense to me. They had been to school together. They had been friends. I turned the machine off and tried to sleep: 0,1,1,2,3,5,8,13,21,34,55,89 ......

I woke at two that morning, sat bolt upright in bed. It was obvious. I dressed quickly, just my grubby clothes from the USA. I'm afraid I ponged a bit but so what? My bike was still intact. I pumped up the tyres, found the lights and set off at racing speed for Peter's house. I don't know what I meant to do when I got there, just that I had to go.

When I was about 50 metres from the house I stopped and stared. All the lights were out. I hid my bike in the rhododendron bushes at the front, then slipped into the back garden. I don't know why, perhaps it was just for old time's sake. I wanted to see how they had kept the lawn in my absence. To my annoyance, as far as I could see, because there was only a splattering of moonlight, the lawn was immaculate, *'no-one's indispensable kid'* a Cutter saying.

Then I saw some lights in the Summer House at the end of the lawn. They called it a Summer House but honestly you could fit a family of four in it quite comfortably. I crept along the edge of the garden, careful not to make a noise. Then I heard Peters. He was laughing. He said something and Lily replied. They were up late. There was a third person with them. I could make that out from the silhouettes but not who it was, so I came closer. My heart beating madly.

Then the third person spoke, a familiar voice with a slight American twang. I knew who it was, of course, obvious really. I'm sure you've guessed. I stood up, walked to the Summer House door, and opened it. The three were sitting round a table, drinking champagne. They looked up at me, mouths open. Honestly it was funny.

'What are you all looking so shocked for?', I said, 'I'm not the one supposed to be dead here.'

It was Cutter who broke the silence, 'you always were a smart kid.'

'Glad to see you're still with us Sam. How did you do it?'

'Smoke and mirrors Zac, just smoke and mirrors.'

Lilly stood up, kissed me on the cheek, 'would you like to a glass of champagne Zac?'

'It's a bit too early in the morning for me but in the circumstances, yes please.'

'It's Poulet Roger,' said Peters

'My favourite,' I said, although I'd never had champagne in

my life, never mind one named after a French chicken called Roger, 'so you played me then? Were you all in it?'

'I'm afraid we were,' said Lilly.

'Just a big act?' I felt that familiar dread entering my stomach. No-one ever liked me for myself I was just a burden, case work, a problem. Someone to whom people were professionally concerned.

Cutters and Peter looked at each other. Peters spoke up, 'no it wasn't an act Zac. We nearly called the whole thing off then you just jumped ahead. The investment scheme was just about to fold. Your move saved us £25M. There was nothing we could do but let the game play out. Sorry.'

'A game?' I said.

'Your Dad and I were close friends. It was like being with him again. I'm glad you're in the know now. We can be mates again.'

'I would like that too,' said Lilly, 'family.'

'Ari know about this?' I asked.

'No, and she never must,' said Peters firmly, 'although she now knows what the family is.'

'There are layers of lies we all operate in,' piped up Cutter.

'So not quite family then,' I said.

'We all have our role to play, 'said Lilly, 'as I taught you.'

'A family of crooks?'

'You in or not?' asked Cutter in his usual blunt manner, 'You have to play by our rules though?'

I stood up, raised my glass, 'I'm in'. This was the only family that had ever really wanted me or shown an interest in me. I wasn't going to let them go.

They cheered and we clinked glasses. I took a sip and it made me splutter.

'An acquired taste is champagne. Believe me some of the biggest crooks in history have drunk this stuff. Welcome to the Family.'

They sent me to Malhangers, and that was how I came to be sitting in the welcoming assembly for year twelve. It had been a blast.

23

The first month was the most intense of my life. I learned so much, and not just advanced maths and history. One afternoon we heard a brilliant lecture about the latest techniques in cyber-crime. Pumped up afterwards, I went for a run. I wanted to be fit with a razor-sharp mind. I wanted to take on the world that had been so spiteful to me. This was my chance to hit back. I could also get rich at the same time.

The other thing was it was going to be fun, great. I ran for about 10k, music blasting in my ear then, as twilight descended, I came back to the college grounds. I had a quick shower. Everyone else was in the cafeteria but I wasn't hungry. I drifted into the library, switched on a laptop, watched the world news. I wanted to find out what was going on out there in the real world, maybe send a few e-mails to Paul, maybe not. He didn't really want me. I'd got in his way. He preferred Sharon.

Then it caught my eye, a small piece about Singular Dynamic, SD. I clicked on it and read through the article. It was about the collapse of the fund, the disappearance and probable death of Cutter. As I speed read down the page, a paragraph jumped out on me. It was about an elderly couple who had lost their life savings and were now surviving on hand-outs. One man, left with nothing, had committed suicide. He wasn't the only one. Many had lost their jobs and were unemployed Several people had to sell their homes and had family breakdowns, divorces, separations. There wasn't just one like that, there were hundreds of them, thousands. Then it really hit me. I don't know why it had taken so long for me to realise. It had been, for me, all about the numbers, abstract, figures on a computer screen - red and black, mostly red: but this were real because there were victims, people were suffering. Crime was never victimless and financial crime, particularly cyber, could touch the lives of thousands of people.

I know I hadn't been responsible for SD, but I'd taken a part, even if I'd been unwittingly played at the time. Then I'd benefited from it. I'd joined the Family. Something snapped inside me. It was as if I had been in a dream and had just woken up. Only I'd woken up into a nightmare, because now I was trusted. I was in the Family. but Peters or Cutter weren't my father. I didn't have a father, even when he was alive my own dad was no good for me. What had I been thinking about? Now I was at Malhangers I could never really escape. I was one of them. but I knew suddenly, deep down I wasn't really. I found myself having a panic attack. I started counting again. Good old Fibonacci. I hadn't met up with him for a while – 1,1,2,3,5,8,13,21,34,55,89,144 ...

I worked my way up the steps to the roof top fire exit and forced open the door. There was a flat area, which we weren't meant to visit, some students had been caught up there once, totally stoned. It was a miracle no-one had fallen off. After that it was off limits. But this was a school to teach us how to break the rules, and get away with it, right? Only I didn't want to break the rules, I just wanted an end to it all. I was trapped in this for life. I had suddenly realised that and now there was no way out. I stepped to the edge of the roof and looked down. It was a long way and would do the trick. It would be quick and not so painful. Nobody would grieve for me for long. I didn't really have anyone. It would be hushed up, the coroner's verdict "accidental death". But I knew that this was never going to be the solution. I'd be bound to change my mind halfway down and what could I do about it? **Suicide took away the possibility of anything going right, ever.**

'Zac, what are you doing?'

It was Ari's voice.

'Don't go any further,' she said.

I felt her hand on my arm, pulling me back. I turned to look at her. She'd been crying.

'I'm so sorry Zac, that you were drawn into this. I didn't know myself, until my Dad told me, just before we came here. I wheedled it out of him.'

'Are you having doubts too?' I asked.

'I don't have any doubts at all Zac, none. This place. These people. It's just wrong.'

We sat down together, our backs against the wall. We put our arms around each other's shoulders. I tried to kiss her. She pulled away.

'Sorry'

She smiled, turned to look at me, 'what are we going to do?'

I thought for a few minutes, watching the night sky getting darker. 'I don't know.'

'Remember that time when we worked on that problem at home, and you said to me "sometimes there is no solution to a problem". Do you remember that?' she said.

I nodded.

'Well, we haven't tried looking for a solution yet, have we? Not properly.'

Then I knew there was hope. Ari and I would find a way forward, but it just wouldn't be easy. Meanwhile, it was a lovely star lit sky and I was sitting next to a beautiful girl, so it wasn't all rubbish, was it?

Printed in Great Britain
by Amazon

74623463R00058